TALES OF CÚ CHULAIND

IRISH HEROIC MYTHS

TRANSLATED BY JEFFREY GANTZ

PENGUIN BOOKS

PENGUIN BOOKS

Published by the Penguin Group
Penguin Books Ltd, 27 Wrights Lane, London w8 5tz, England
Penguin Books USA Inc., 375 Hudson Street, New York, New York 10014, USA
Penguin Books Australia Ltd, Ringwood, Victoria, Australia
Penguin Books Canada Ltd, 10 Alcorn Avenue, Toronto, Ontario, Canada m4v 3b2
Penguin Books (NZ) Ltd, 182–190 Wairau Road, Auckland 10, New Zealand

Penguin Books Ltd, Registered Offices: Harmondsworth, Middlesex, England

These stories are from Jeffrey Gantz's translation of *Early Irish Myths and Sagas*,
first published in Penguin Classics 1981
This edition published 1996
1 3 5 7 9 10 8 6 4 2

Translation copyright © Jeffrey Gantz, 1981
All rights reserved

The moral right of the translator has been asserted

Printed in England by Clays Ltd, St Ives plc

CONTENTS

The Birth of Cú Chulaind

One time, when Conchubur and the chieftains of Ulaid* were at Emuin Machae, a flock of birds frequented the plain outside Emuin, and it grazed there until not so much as a root or a stalk or a blade of grass remained. The Ulaid were distressed to see the land so devastated, and thus, one day, they harnessed nine chariots and set out to drive the birds away, for it was their custom to hunt birds. Conchubur sat in his chariot together with his grown sister Deichtine, for she was his charioteer; and the other champions of the Ulaid sat in their chariots, Conall and Lóegure and everyone else, even Bricriu. Before them the birds flew, over Slíab Fúait, over Edmund, over Brega, and the Ulaid were enchanted by the birds' flight and by their singing. There were nine score birds in all, each score flying separately, and each pair of birds was linked by a silver chain.

Towards evening three birds broke away and made for Bruig na Bóinde. Then night came upon the Ulaid, and a great snow fell, so Conchubur told his people to unyoke their chariots, and he sent a party to seek shelter. Conall and Bricriu searched the area and found a single house, new; they went inside and were welcomed by the couple there, and then they returned to their people. Bricriu complained that it would not be worthwhile to go to a house that had neither food nor

* Ulster people.

clothing and was narrow into the bargain. All the same, the Ulaid went; they took their chariots with them, but they did not take much inside. Suddenly, they discovered a storehouse door before them. Then it came time to eat, and the Ulaid grew merry with drink, and their disposition was good. The man of the house told them that his wife was in labour in the storehouse, so Deichtine went back to help, and soon a son was born. At the same time, a mare that was at the entrance to the house gave birth to two foals. The Ulaid gave the colts to the boy as a gift, and Deichtine nursed him.

When morning came, the Ulaid found themselves east of the Bruig – no house, no birds, only their horses and the boy with his colts. They returned to Emuin Machae, and the boy was nursed until he was a young lad, but then he fell ill and died. Tears were shed, and Deichtine was greatly saddened by the death of her foster-son. Finally, when she had left off sighing, she felt thirsty and she requested drink from a copper vessel, and that was brought. Every time she put the vessel to her mouth, a tiny creature would leap from the liquid towards her lips; yet, when she took the vessel from her mouth, there was nothing to be seen. That night, she had a dream: a man spoke to her and said that he had brought her towards the Bruig, that it was his house she had entered, that she was pregnant by him and that it was a son that would be born. The man's name was Lug son of Eithliu; the boy's name was to be Sétantae, and it was for him that the colts were to be reared.

Thereafter, Deichtine indeed became pregnant. The Ulaid were troubled since they did not know the father, and they surmised that Conchubur had fathered the child while drunk, for Deichtine used to sleep next to him. Conchubur then betrothed his sister to Súaltaim son of Roech. Deichtine was greatly embarrassed at having to go to Súaltaim's bed while being pregnant, so, when the time came, she lay down in the bed and crushed the child within her. Then she went to Súaltaim, and at once she became pregnant by him and bore him a son.

The Boyhood Deeds of Cú Chulaind

'In truth, he was reared by his mother and his father at Airgdech in Mag Muirthemni,' said Fergus. 'There he was told of the fame of the boys at Emuin Machae, for three fifties of boys play there. Conchubur enjoys his sovereignty thus: one third of the day watching the boys play, one third playing fidchell* and one third drinking until he falls asleep. Although we are in exile because of him, there is not in Ériu a greater warrior.

'Cú Chulaind entreated his mother, then, to let him go to the boys. "You are not to go," she replied, "until one of the champions of Ulaid can accompany you." "Too long to wait, that," Cú Chulaind answered. "Just tell me in which direction Emuin lies." "To the north, there, and the path is dangerous," said his mother. "Slíab Fúait lies between you and Emuin." "Even so, I will try it," said Cú Chulaind. He went forth, then, with his toy javelin and his toy shield and his hurley and his ball. He would throw his javelin on ahead and then catch it before it could strike the ground.

'When he reached Emuin, he went to the boys without first securing their protection – at that time, no one went to the playing field without a guarantee that the boys would protect him. Cú Chulaind was unaware of this. "The boy outrages us," said Follomon son of Conchubur, "and yet we know he

* A board game, similar to chess.

is of the Ulaid." The boys warned Cú Chulaind off, but he defeated them. They threw their three fifties of javelins at him, but he stopped every one with his toy shield. They threw their three fifties of balls at him, but he caught them all against his chest. They threw their three fifties of hurleys at him, but he warded them off and took an armful on his back.

'Then his ríastarthae* came upon him. You would have thought that every hair was being driven into his head. You would have thought that a spark of fire was on every hair. He closed one eye until it was no wider than the eye of a needle; he opened the other until it was as big as a wooden bowl. He bared his teeth from jaw to ear, and he opened his mouth until the gullet was visible. The warrior's moon rose from his head.

'Cú Chulaind struck at the boys and overthrew fifty of them before they could reach the doors of Emuin. Nine of them ran over Conchubur and myself as we were playing fidchell; Cú Chulaind sprang over the board after them, but Conchubur took his arm and said, "Not good your treatment of the boy troop." "Fair play it is," answered Cú Chulaind. "I came from my mother and my father to play with them, and they were not nice to me." "What is your name?" asked Conchubur. "Sétantae, the son of Súaltaim and of Deichtine, your sister. I did not expect such a reception here." "Why did you not secure the boys' protection?" asked Conchubur. "I did not know that was necessary," replied Cú Chulaind. "Accept my protection now, then," said Conchubur. "That I will," answered Cú Chulaind.

* Battle fury.

5

'That same day Cú Chulaind turned upon the boys in the house. "What is wrong with you now?" asked Conchubur. "I wish that their protection be given over to me," Cú Chulaind answered. "Undertake to protect them, then," said Conchubur. "That I will," replied Cú Chulaind.

'They returned to the playing field, then, and those boys who had been struck down arose, and their foster-mothers and foster-fathers helped them.'

'Another time, there was a falling out between the Ulaid and Éogan son of Durthacht. The Ulaid went into battle while Cú Chulaind was still asleep; they were defeated, but Conchubur and Cúscraid Mend Machae and a great multitude survived, and their wailing woke him. He stretched so that the two stones on either side of him broke – this in the presence of Bricriu yonder – and then he arose. I met him at the courtyard entrance, I being wounded. "Alas! God preserve your life, popa Fergus," he said. "Where is Conchubur?" "I do not know," I answered.

'He set off, then, into the dark night. He made for the battlefield, and there he found a man with half a head, and half of another man on his back. "Help me, Cú Chulaind," the man said, "for I have been wounded, and I have half my brother on my back. Carry him a while with me." "That I will not," replied Cú Chulaind. The man put his burden on Cú Chulaind's back; Cú Chulaind threw it off. They wrestled, and Cú Chulaind was thrown. He heard the Badb* from among the corpses: "A bad warrior he who lies at the feet of a

---

* Goddess of war, haunter of battlefields.

6

spectre." Cú Chulaind rose to attack the man, then; he struck his head off with his hurley and drove it before him across the plain.

'"Is popa Conchubur in this battlefield?" Cú Chulaind asked, and his question was answered. He went on until he found Conchubur in a ditch, with dirt piled up about him on every side. "Why did you come to the battlefield and the mortal terror that is here?" asked Conchubur. Cú Chulaind raised Conchubur up out of the ditch – six Ulaid champions could not have raised him more bravely. "Bear me to that house yonder," Conchubur said, "and light me a great fire there." Cú Chulaind lit the fire. "Good, that," said Conchubur. "Now if I were to get a roasted pig to eat, I would live." Cú Chulaind went out and found a man over a cooking spit in the middle of the forest, one hand holding his weapons, the other cooking a boar. The man was terrifying; even so, Cú Chulaind attacked and took the man's head and the boar. Conchubur ate the pig, after which he said, "Let us go to our own house." On the way they met Cúscraid son of Conchubur; he was badly wounded, so Cú Chulaind carried him on his back, and the three returned to Emuin Machae.'

'We knew that boy, indeed,' said Conall Cernach, 'and we were none the worse for knowing him. He was our fosterling. Not long after the deeds Fergus has just related he performed another feat.

'When Culand the smith offered Conchubur his hospitality, he asked that a large host should not come, for the feast would be the fruit not of lands and possessions but of his tongs and his two hands. Conchubur went with fifty of his

7

oldest and most illustrious heroes in their chariots. First, however, he visited the playing field, for it was his custom when leaving or returning to seek the boys' blessing; and he saw Cú Chulaind driving the ball past the three fifties of boys and defeating them. When they drove at the hole, Cú Chulaind filled the hole with his balls, and the boys could not stop them; when the boys drove at the hole, he defended it alone, and not a single ball went in. When they wrestled, he overthrew the three fifties of boys by himself, but all of them together could not overthrow him. When they played at mutual stripping, he stripped them all so that they were stark naked, while they could not take so much as the brooch from his mantle.

'Conchubur thought all this wonderful. He asked if the boy's deeds would be similarly distinguished when he became a man, and everyone said that they would be. He said to Cú Chulaind, then, "Come with me to the feast, and you will be a guest." "I have not had my fill of play yet," replied the boy. "I will come after you."

'When everyone had arrived at the feast, Culand said to Conchubur, "Do you expect anyone else?" "I do not," answered Conchubur, forgetting that his fosterling was yet to come. "I have a watchdog," said Culand, "with three chains on him and three men on every chain. I will loose him now to guard our cattle and our herds, and I will close the courtyard."

'By that time, the boy was on his way to the feast, and when the hound attacked him he was still at play. He would throw his ball up and his hurley after it, so that the hurley struck the ball and so that each stroke was the same; he would also throw his javelin on ahead and catch it before it could strike the ground. The hound's attack did not distract the boy from his play; Conchubur and his people, however, were so confounded that they could not move. They could not believe that, when the courtyard doors were opened, they would find the boy alive. But, when the hound attacked him, the boy threw away his ball and hurley and went at it with his bare hands: he put one hand on the hound's throat and the other on its back and struck it against a pillar until every limb fell apart.

'The Ulaid rose to rescue him, some to the courtyard and some to the door of the courtyard, and they took him in to Conchubur. Everyone was greatly alarmed that the son of the king's sister had nearly been killed. But Culand entered the house and said, "Welcome, lad, for the sake of your mother's heart. As for myself, however, this was an evil feast. My life is lost, and my household are out on the plain, without our hound. It secured life and honour; it protected our goods and cattle and every creature between field and house. It was the man of the family." "No great matter, that," replied the boy. "I will rear you a whelp from the same litter, and, until it has grown and is capable of action, I will be the hound that protects your cattle and yourself. I will protect all Mag Muirthemni, and neither herd nor flock will be taken without my knowledge." "Cú Chulaind will be your name henceforth," said Cathub. "I prefer my own name," said Cú Chulaind.*

'The boy who did that when he was six would not surprise

* 'Sétantae', his name at birth, means 'one who has knowledge of roads and ways'. 'Cú Chulaind' means 'the Hound of Culand'.

by doing heroic deeds when he was seventeen,' said Conall Cernach.

'There were other deeds as well,' said Fíachu son of Fer Febe. 'Cathub the druid was with his son, Conchubur son of Ness, and he was teaching one hundred men the druid's art, for that is the number he used to instruct. One pupil asked him what that day would be good for, and he said that a warrior who took arms that day would be famous among the men of Ériu and that stories of him would be told for ever.

'When Cú Chulaind heard that, he went to Conchubur to ask for arms. "Who instructed you?" Conchubur asked. "My tutor, Cathub," Cú Chulaind replied. "Indeed, we know him," said Conchubur. He gave Cú Chulaind a spear and shield, but Cú Chulaind shook them in the centre of the house until none of the fifteen spare sets of weapons in Conchubur's household escaped being broken or taken away. He was given Conchubur's own weapons, then; these endured him, and he shook them and saluted Conchubur and said, "Happy the race and the people whose king has such weapons."

'Cathub went to Conchubur, then, and said, "Is the boy taking arms?" "He is," answered Conchubur. "Ill luck, then, for his mother's son," said Cathub, but Conchubur replied, "Why? Did you not instruct him to take arms?" "Indeed, I did not," answered Cathub. Then Conchubur said to Cú Chulaind, "Why did you lie to me, sprite?" "No lie, king of the Féni.* He was instructing his students this morning, and I heard him to the south of Emuin, and thus I came to you,"

---

* The Irish.

answered Cú Chulaind. "A good day, then," said Cathub, "for he who takes arms today will be great and famous – and short-lived." "Wonderful news, that," answered Cú Chulaind, "for, if I am famous, I will be happy even to live just one day."

'The next morning, another pupil asked the druids what that day would be good for. "Anyone who steps into a chariot today," Cathub replied, "will be known to the Ériu for ever." When Cú Chulaind heard that, he went to Conchubur and said, "Popa Conchubur, a chariot for me!" Conchubur gave him a chariot, but when Cú Chulaind put his hand between the two chariot poles, it broke. He broke twelve chariots that way, so Conchubur's own chariot was brought for him, and that endured.

'Cú Chulaind went off in the chariot, taking Conchubur's charioteer along with him. The charioteer – Ibor was his name – turned the chariot about, saying, "Come out of the chariot, now." But Cú Chulaind replied, "The horses are beautiful, and I am beautiful, lad. Take a turn round Emuin with us, and I will reward you." After that, Cú Chulaind made Ibor take him to say goodbye to the boys, "so that the boys might bless me." He entreated the charioteer to return to the road, and when they arrived he said, "Put the whip to the horses, now." "In what direction?" asked Ibor. "As far as the road leads," Cú Chulaind answered.

'They went on to Slíab Fúait, where they met Conall Cernach. That day it was Conall's turn to protect the province – every Ulaid warrior of worth took a turn at Slíab Fúait, protecting those who came with poems, fighting enemies and seeing that no one came to Emuin unannounced. "May you prosper," said Conall, "and may you be victorious and triumphant." "Return to the fort, Conall, and leave me here to watch in your place," said Cú Chulaind. "Well enough, that," said Conall, "for protecting those with poetry, but you are not yet able to fight." "Perhaps it will not come to that," said Cú Chulaind. "In any case, let us go to look at the sandbar at Loch nEchtrae, for it is customary for young warriors to rest there." "Very well," replied Conall.

'They started out, but Cú Chulaind cast a stone from his sling and broke Conall's chariot pole. "Why did you cast that stone, little boy?" asked Conall. "To test my hand and the straightness of my cast," answered Cú Chulaind. "It is an Ulaid custom not to drive through danger – therefore return to Emuin, popa Conall, and leave me here to watch." "All right, then," said Conall, and he did not drive across the plain after that.

'Cú Chulaind drove off to Loch nEchtrae, then, but he found no one there. Ibor told him they should return to Emuin and drink, but Cú Chulaind replied, "By no means. What mountain is that yonder?" "Slíab Monduirn," Ibor told him. "Let us travel until we reach it," Cú Chulaind said. They drove to Slíab Monduirn, and when they arrived Cú Chulaind asked, "What is that white cairn yonder on the upper part of the mountain?" "Findcharn." "What is the plain yonder?" "Mag mBreg." Ibor then told him the name of every major fort between Temuir and Cenandas; moreover, he identified the meadows and fords, the dwellings and illustrious places, the forts and the great heights. He pointed out the fort of the three sons of Nechta Scéne: Foill and Fannall and Túachell. "Is it they who say that there are not more of the Ulaid alive than they have slain?" asked Cú Chulaind. "It is they," replied Ibor. "Let us go on, then, until we meet them," said Cú Chulaind. "Dangerous, that, indeed," said the charioteer. "Not to avoid danger have we come," said Cú Chulaind.

'They went on, then, and unyoked the horses at Cómbor Manae and Abae to the south and above the fort. Cú Chulaind took the spancel that was around the pillar and threw it into the river and let the water carry it, for such an action was a breach of geiss* to the sons of Nechta Scéne. The sons perceived what he had done and started out to meet him, but Cú Chulaind went to sleep against the pillar, first saying to Ibor, "Do not wake me just for a few but only for a large crowd." Ibor was very frightened; he yoked the chariot and tugged at its skins and coverings, which Cú Chulaind was sleeping on, but he dared not wake the boy since Cú Chulaind had said he was to wake him only for a great crowd.

'The sons of Nechta Scéne arrived, then, and one of them asked, "What is this?" "A little boy making an expedition in his chariot," replied Ibor. "Neither prosperous nor auspicious, this first taking of arms," said the warrior. "Let him leave this land, and let his horses not graze here any more." "I have the reins in my hand," said Ibor. "You have no reason to incur the enmity of the Ulaid – besides, the boy is asleep." "Indeed, he is not a boy at all," said Cú Chulaind, "but a lad who has come in search of combat." "My pleasure," said Foill. "Let it be your pleasure, then, in the ford yonder," said Cú Chulaind.

'"You must take note of the man who comes to meet you,"

---

* A bond, taboo or magical injunction, the violation of which led to misfortune or death.

Ibor told Cú Chulaind. "Foill is his name, and if you do not reach him with the first thrust, you will not reach him at all." Cú Chulaind answered, "I swear by the god my people swear by, he will not play that trick upon the Ulaid after my father Conchubur's broad-pointed spear has reached him. An enemy hand, mine." Cú Chulaind cast his spear at Foill and broke his back and took his head and his weapons.

'"Take heed of the next man, now," said Ibor. "Fannall his name, and he treads upon the water as lightly as would a swan or a swallow." "I swear by the god my people swear by, he will not play that trick upon the Ulaid again. Indeed, you have seen how I tread upon the pool at Emuin." They met at the ford; Cú Chulaind slew Fannall and took his head and his weapons.

'"Take heed now of the last man," said Ibor. "Túachell his name, and no mistake, for arms will not fell him." "Here, then, the del chliss* to confound him and make a sieve of him." Cú Chulaind cast his spear at Túachell, and the latter's limbs collapsed; he went and struck Túachell's head off and gave the head and spoils to Ibor. They heard the wailing of the sons' mother, Nechta Scéne, behind them, but Cú Chulaind took the spoils and the three heads with him into the chariot, saying, "I will not abandon my triumph until I reach Emuin Machae."

'They set off with their victory, and Cú Chulaind said to Ibor, "You promised me a good drive, and we need that now because of the pursuit behind us." They drove on to Slíab Fúait, and, with Ibor whipping, they went so fast that the

* Spear-thrusting feat.

horses overtook the wind and birds in flight, so fast that Cú Chulaind was able to catch a cast from his sling before it could strike the ground. When they reached Slíab Fúait, they found a herd of deer before them. "What beasts are these that are so nimble?" asked Cú Chulaind. "Deer," replied the charioteer. "Would the Ulaid think it better to bring them back dead or alive?" asked Cú Chulaind. "Alive, for not everyone could do that, but all can bring them back dead. But you are not capable of bringing any back alive," said the charioteer. "Indeed, I am," replied Cú Chulaind. "Whip the horses and drive them into the bog." Ibor did that; the horses stuck fast in the bog, and Cú Chulaind leapt out and seized the nearest, finest deer. He lashed the horses out of the bog, then, and tamed the deer immediately and bound it between the chariot poles.

'After that, they saw a flock of swans before them. "Would the Ulaid think it better to bring these back dead or alive?" asked Cú Chulaind. "The bravest and most accomplished warriors bring them back alive," answered the charioteer. Cú Chulaind aimed a small stone at the birds and brought down eight of them; he took a large stone, then, and brought down twelve more, with a stunning blow. "Collect the birds now," he said to the charioteer, "for if I go myself, the deer will spring upon you." "Indeed, it will not be easy for me to go," replied Ibor, "for the horses have become so wild I cannot go past them. I cannot go past the two iron wheels of the chariot because of their sharpness, and I cannot go past the deer because its horns have filled the space between the chariot poles." "Step out on its antlers, then," said Cú Chulaind, "for I swear by the god the Ulaid swear by, I will turn my head and fix the deer with my eye so that it will not turn its head to you or dare to move.'' They did that: Cú Chulaind held the reins fast, and Ibor collected the birds. Cú Chulaind then bound the birds with strings and cords from the chariot so that as they drove to Emuin Machae the deer was behind the chariot, the three heads were in the chariot and the swans were flying overhead.

'When they arrived at Emuin, the watchman said, "A man in a chariot is approaching, and he will shed the blood of every person here unless naked women are sent to meet him.'' Cú Chulaind turned the left side of his chariot towards Emuin, and that was a geiss to the fort; he said, "I swear by the god the Ulaid swear by, unless a man is found to fight me, I will shed the blood of everyone in the fort.'' "Naked women to meet him!'' shouted Conchubur. The women of Emuin went to meet Cú Chulaind gathered round Mugain, Conchubur's wife, and they bared their breasts before him. "These are the warriors who will meet you today!'' said Mugain. Cú Chulaind hid his face, whereupon the warriors of Ulaid seized him and thrust him into a vat of cold water. The vat burst, but the second vat into which he was thrust boiled up with fist-sized bubbles, and the third vat he merely heated to a moderate warmth. When he left the third vat, the queen, Mugain, placed about him a blue mantle with a silver brooch and a hooded tunic. He sat at Conchubur's knee, then, and that was his bed ever after. The man who did this in his seventh year,' said Fíachu son of Fer Febe, 'no wonder should he prevail against odds or demolish an equal opponent now that he is seventeen.'

The Death of Aífe's Only Son

Cú Chulaind went to study weaponry with Scáthach nÚanaind daughter of Airdgeme so that he might master feats. Aífe daughter of Airdgeme went to him there, and when she left she was pregnant, and he told her that she would bear a son. 'You are to keep this golden thumb ring,' he said, 'until the boy can wear it. When that time comes, let him follow me to Ériu. Let him turn aside for no one, and let him identify himself to no one, and let him refuse to fight no one.'

After seven years the boy went to seek his father. The Ulaid were assembled at Trácht Éise, and they saw the boy out on the sea, in a bronze ship, with golden oars in his hands. He had a heap of stones in the boat, and he placed these in his slingshot and dealt stunning blows to the birds overhead, so that the creatures were knocked unconscious; afterwards he revived them and sent them back to the air. He performed the jaw feat with his hands until his upper jaw reached his eye. After that he modulated his voice until he had laid the birds low a second time, and he revived them a second time as well.

'Woe, indeed,' said Conchubur, 'to the land to which yonder lad comes. If the great men from his island were to arrive, they would pound us to dust, inasmuch as a mere boy performs such feats. Let someone go to meet him, and let him not enter this country.' 'Who should go to meet him?' 'Who but Condere son of Echu,' answered Conchubur. 'Why should Condere go?' asked everyone. 'Not difficult, that,' replied Conchubur.

'Whatever good sense and eloquence may be required, Condere will possess it.' 'I will go to meet him,' said Condere. Condere went, then, and he met the boy as the latter came ashore. 'Far enough, that, little boy, until you tell us where you come from and who your family is.' 'I will not identify myself to any man,' said the boy, 'and I will not turn aside for any man.' 'You will not enter this country until you have identified yourself,' said Condere. 'I will continue the journey on which I have come,' said the boy.

The boy turned away, then, but Condere said, 'Turn to me, my boy. You are capable of great deeds. You are the stuff of blood. The pride of the warriors of Ulaid is in you. Conchubur welcomes you. Your jaws and spears away from the left side of your chariot, lest the warriors of Ulaid rise against you. Conchubur invites you to come to us. An ear for you if you turn towards me. Come to Conchubur, the impetuous son of Ness; to Senchae, the victorious son of Ailill; to Cethernd of the red sword edge, the son of Findtan, with a fire that wounds battalions; to Amorgen the poet; to Cúscraid of the great hosts. I welcome you; Conall Cernach invites you to stories, songs and the laughter of war heroes. Blaí Briugu would be greatly distressed if you journeyed on past him, he being a hero; moreover, to shame so many is not right. I, Condere, arose to meet the boy who detains champions. I vowed that I would meet this boy, though he has neither beard nor manly hair, provided he is not disobedient to the Ulaid.'

'Good your coming,' said the boy, 'for now you will have your conversation. I have modulated my voice. I have left off casting unerringly from chariots. I have collected a beautiful flight of birds by shooting far-flying little spears at them, and moreover without the hero's salmon leap. I have vowed great feats of arms lest anyone lay siege against me. Go and ask the Ulaid whether they wish to come against me singly or in a host. Turn back, now, for, even if you had the strength of a hundred, you would not be worthy to detain me.'

'Let someone else come to talk with you, then,' said Condere. He returned to the Ulaid and repeated the conversation, and Conall Cernach said, 'The Ulaid will not be shamed while I am alive.' He went to meet the boy, saying, 'Delightful your games, little boy.' 'They will not be any the less so for you,' answered the boy. He placed a stone in his slingshot and delivered a stunning blow; the thunder and shock of it knocked Conall head over heels, and before he could rise, the boy had taken the strap from his shield. Conall returned to the Ulaid and said, 'Someone else to meet him!'; but the rest of the host only smiled.

Cú Chulaind, however, was approaching the boy, playing, with the arm of Emer daughter of Forgall round his neck. 'Do not go down there!' she said. 'It is your son who is there. Do not slaughter your son, O impetuous, well-bred lad. Neither fair nor right is it to rise against your son of great and valorous deeds. Turn away from the skin-torment of the sapling of your tree; remember Scáthach's warning. If Condlae sustained the left board, there would be a fierce combat. Turn to me! Listen! My advice is good! Let it be Cú Chulaind who listens. I know what name he bears, if that is Condlae the only son of Aífe who is below.' But Cú Chulaind answered, 'Silence, woman! It is not a woman's advice I seek regarding deeds of bright splendour. Such deeds are not performed with a woman's assistance. Let us be triumphant in feats. Sated the eyes of a great king. A mist of blood upon my skin the gore from the body of Condlae. Beautifully spears will suck the fair javelin. Whatever were down there, woman, I would go for the sake of the Ulaid.'

Cú Chulaind went down to the shore, then. 'Delightful your games, little boy,' he said, but Condlae answered, 'Not delightful the game you play, for no two of you will come unless I identify myself.' 'Must I have a little boy in my presence? You will die unless you identify yourself.' 'Prove that,' said the boy. He rose towards Cú Chulaind, then, and the two of them struck at each other; the boy performed the hair-cutting feat with his sword and left Cú Chulaind bald. 'The mockery is at an end. Let us wrestle,' Cú Chulaind said. 'I would not reach your belt,' answered the boy. But he stood upon two pillars and threw Cú Chulaind down between the pillars three times; he moved neither of his feet, so that they went into the stone up to his ankles.

They went to wrestle in the water, then, and the boy ducked Cú Chulaind twice. After that, Cú Chulaind rose out of the water and deceived the boy with the gáe bolga,* for Scáthach had never taught that weapon to anyone but Cú Chulaind. He cast it at the boy through the water, and the boy's innards fell at his feet.

'That,' said the boy, 'is what Scáthach did not teach me. Alas that you have wounded me!' 'True, that,' said Cú Chulaind, and he took the boy in his arms and carried him up from the shore and showed him to the Ulaid, saying, 'Here is

* Another spear-thrusting feat.

my son.' 'Alas, indeed,' they said. 'True enough,' said the boy, 'for, had I stayed among you five years, I would have slain men on all sides, and you would have possessed kingdoms as far distant as Rome. Now show me the great men who dwell here, that I may take my leave of them.' He put his arms round the neck of each man in turn, then, and bade his father farewell and died. Cries of grief were raised, and his grave and marker were made, and for three days not a calf of the cattle of the Ulaid was left alive after him.

The Wasting Sickness of Cú Chulaind
and The Only Jealousy of Emer

Each year the Ulaid held an assembly: the three days before
Samuin and the three days after Samuin* and Samuin itself.
They would gather at Mag Muirthemni, and during these
seven days there would be nothing but meetings and games
and amusements and entertainments and eating and feasting. That is why the thirds of Samuin are as they are
today.

Thus, the Ulaid were assembled at Mag Muirthemni. Now
the reason they met every Samuin was to give each warrior an
opportunity to boast of his valour and exhibit his triumphs.
The warriors put the tongues of those they had killed into
pouches – some threw in cattle tongues to augment the count
– and then, at the assembly, each man spoke in turn and
boasted of his triumphs. They spoke with their swords on
their thighs, swords that turned against anyone who swore
falsely.

Now there had come to this particular assembly every man
but two: Conall Cernach and Fergus son of Roech. 'Let the
assembly be convened,' said the Ulaid. Cú Chulaind, however,
protested, saying, 'Not until Conall and Fergus come', for
Conall was his foster-brother and Fergus his foster-father. So
Senchae said, 'Let us play fidchell and have the poets recite
and the acrobats perform.'

* i.e. 1 November, first day of winter and first day of the new year,
traditionally a day of great change.

While they were at their amusements, a flock of birds settled on the lake, and no flock in Ériu was more beautiful. The women grew very excited over these birds and began to argue over who should have them. Eithne Attencháithrech,* Conchubur's wife, said, 'I desire a bird for each shoulder', but the women replied, 'We all want that too.' 'If anyone is to have them, I should,' said Eithne Ingubai, the wife of Cú Chulaind. 'What will we do?' asked the women. 'Not difficult,' said Lebarcham, the daughter of Óa and Adarc. 'I will go and ask Cú Chulaind.'

She went to Cú Chulaind, then, and said, 'The women desire those birds from you.' But he seized his sword to ply against her, saying, 'Have the sluts of Ulaid nothing better for us than to hunt their birds?' 'Indeed, you ought not to be angry with them,' answered Lebarcham, 'for you are the cause of their third blemish.' The women of Ulaid suffered three blemishes: every woman who loved Conall had a crooked neck; every woman who loved Cúscraid Mend Machae son of Conchubur stammered; and every woman who loved Cú Chulaind blinded in one eye in his likeness. It was Cú Chulaind's gift, when he was angry, that he could withdraw one eye so far into his head that a heron could not reach it, whereas the other eye he could protrude until it was as large as a cauldron for a yearling calf.

'Yoke the chariot for us, Lóeg,' said Cú Chulaind. Lóeg did that, and Cú Chulaind sprang into the chariot, and he dealt

---

* The text of these tales is a conflation of several versions, so Cú Chulaind's wife appears variously as 'Eithne Ingubai' and 'Emer'; Conchubur's wife appears as 'Mugain' and 'Eithne Attencháithrech'.

the birds such a stunning blow with his sword that claws and wings floated in the water. Then he returned with the birds and distributed them so that each woman had a pair – each woman save Eithne Ingubai. When he came to his wife, he said, 'Angry you are.' 'I am not,' she replied, 'for it is by me that the birds were distributed. You did right, for every one of those women loves you or gives you a share of her love, but I share my love with you alone.' 'Then do not be angry,' said Cú Chulaind. 'When birds come to Mag Muirthemni or the Bóand, you will have the most beautiful pair.'

Not long afterwards, they saw flying over the lake two birds coupled by a red-gold chain; these birds sang a little, and sleep fell upon the host. Cú Chulaind rose to go after them, but Eithne said, 'If you listen to me, you will not go, for those birds possess some kind of power. Other birds can be caught for me.' 'Am I likely to be denied?' answered Cú Chulaind. 'Lóeg, put a stone in my sling.' Lóeg did so and Cú Chulaind cast at the birds, but he missed. 'Alas!' he said. He cast a second stone and missed with that also. 'Now I am doomed,' he said, 'for since the day I first took up arms I have never missed my target.' He threw his javelin, but it only pierced the wing of one bird. The creatures then flew along the water.

Cú Chulaind walked on until he sat down with his back against a stone; he was angry, but then sleep overcame him. While sleeping he saw two women approach: one wore a green cloak and the other a crimson cloak folded five times, and the one in green smiled at him and began to beat him with a horsewhip. The other woman then came and smiled also and struck him in the same fashion, and they beat him for such a long time that there was scarcely any life left in him. Then they left.

The Ulaid perceived the state he was in, and they attempted to rouse him. But Fergus said, 'No! Do not disturb him – it is a vision.' Then Cú Chulaind awoke. 'Who did this to you?' asked the Ulaid, but he was unable to speak. He was taken to his sickbed in An Téte Brecc, and he remained there a year without speaking to anyone.

At the end of that year, just before Samuin, the Ulaid were gathered round Cú Chulaind in the house: Fergus by the wall, Conall Cernach by the bedrail, Lugaid Réoderg by the pillow and Eithne Ingubai at his feet; and, as they were thus, a man entered the house and sat at the foot of the bed. 'What brings you here?' asked Conall Cernach. 'Not difficult, that. If this man were healthy, he would guarantee my safety here; and since he is weak and wounded, his guarantee is that much stronger. So I fear none of you, and it is to speak to him that I have come.' 'Have no fear,' said the Ulaid.

Then the man rose and recited these verses:

> Cú Chulaind, sick as you are,
> waiting will be no help.
> If they were yours, they would heal you,
> the daughters of Áed Abrat.
>
> Standing to the right of Labraid Lúathlám,
> in Mag Crúaich, Lí Ban said,
> 'Fand has expressed her desire
> to lie down with Cú Chulaind:

'"A joyous day it would be
were Cú Chulaind to come to my land.
He would have gold and silver
and plenty of wine to drink.

'"Were he my friend now,
Cú Chulaind son of Súaltaim,
perhaps he could relate what he saw
in his sleep, apart from the host.

'"There at Mag Muirthemni in the south
no misfortune will befall you this Samuin.
I will send Lí Ban to you,
Cú Chulaind, sick as you are."'

'Who are you?' the Ulaid asked. 'I am Óengus son of Áed
Abrat.' said the man, and then he left, and the Ulaid knew
neither whence he had come nor where he had gone. But Cú
Chulaind sat up and spoke. 'About time,' the Ulaid said. 'Tell
us what happened to you.' 'I had a vision last year, at
Samuin,' Cú Chulaind replied, and he related what he had
seen. 'What now, Conchubur?' he asked. 'You must return to
that same stone,' answered Conchubur.

Cú Chulaind walked out then until he reached the stone,
and there he saw the woman in the green cloak. 'Good, this,
Cú Chulaind,' she said. 'Not good for me your journey here
last year,' he replied. 'Not to harm you did we come, but to
seek your friendship. Indeed, I have come to speak to you of
Fand, the daughter of Áed Abrat: Manandán son of Ler has
left her, and she has now given her love to you. My name is Lí
Ban, and I bear a message from my husband, Labraid Lúathlám ar Cladeb: he will send Fand to you in exchange for one

day's fighting against Senach Síaborthe and Echu Íuil and Éogan Indber.' 'Indeed, I am not fit to fight men today,' answered Cú Chulaind. 'That is soon remedied: you will be healed, and your full strength will be restored.' 'Where is this place?' 'In Mag Mell. Now I must return,' said Lí Ban. 'Let Lóeg go with you to visit your land,' said Cú Chulaind. 'Let him come, then,' said Lí Ban.

Lí Ban and Lóeg then went to see Fand. When they arrived, Lí Ban seized Lóeg by the shoulder and said, 'Do not leave this place today, Lóeg, save under a woman's protection.' 'Being protected by women has not exactly been my custom,' replied Lóeg. 'A pity it is not Cú Chulaind who is here now,' moaned Lí Ban. 'I too would rather he were here,' said Lóeg.

They went, then, to the side facing the island, where they saw a bronze boat crossing the lake and coming towards them. They entered the boat and crossed to the island; there, they found a doorway, and a man appeared. Lí Ban asked the man:

> Where is Labraid Lúathlám ar Cladeb,
> head of the troops of victory,
> victory above a steady chariot,
> he who reddens spear points with blood?

The man answered her, saying:

> Labraid is fierce and vigorous;
> he will not be slow, he will have many followers.
> An army is being mustered; if Mag Fidgai is crowded,
> there will be great slaughter.

They entered the house, then, and saw three fifties of couches and three fifties of women lying on them. These women all greeted Lóeg, saying, 'Welcome, Lóeg, for the sake of the woman with whom you have come, and for the sake of the man from whom you have come, and for your own sake.' Lí Ban asked, 'Well, Lóeg? Will you go speak with Fand?' 'I will, provided I know where we are.' 'Not difficult, that – we are in a chamber apart.' They went to speak with Fand, and she welcomed them in the same way. Fand was the daughter of Áed Abrat, that is, fire of eyelash, for the pupil is the fire of the eye. Fand is the tear that covers the eye, and she was so named for her purity and beauty, since there was not her like anywhere in the world.

As they stood there, they heard the sound of Labraid's chariot coming to the island, and Lí Ban said, 'Labraid is angry today. Let us go talk to him.' They went outside, and Lí Ban welcomed Labraid, saying:

> Welcome, Labraid Lúathlám ar Cladeb!
> Heir of troops,
> of swift spearmen,
> he smites shields,
> scatters spears,
> wounds bodies,
> slays free men,
> sees slaughter.
> More beautiful than women,
> he destroys hosts
> and scatters treasures.
> Assailant of a warrior band, welcome!

Labraid did not answer, so Lí Ban spoke on:

> Welcome, Labraid Lúathlám ar Cladeb Augra!
> Prompt to grant requests,

generous to all,
eager for combat.
Battle-scarred his side,
dependable his word,
forceful his justice,
amiable his rule,
skilful his right hand,
vengeful his deeds –
he cuts down warriors.
Welcome, Labraid!

As Labraid still remained silent, Lí Ban recited another poem:

Welcome, Labraid Lúathlám ar Cladeb!
More warlike than youths,
prouder than chieftains,
he destroys valiant adversaries,
fights battalions,
sieves young warriors,
raises up the weak,
lays low the strong.
Welcome, Labraid!

'What you say is not good, woman,' replied Labraid, and he recited this poem:

I am neither proud nor arrogant, woman,
nor is my bearing over-haughty.
We go to a battle with fierce spears everywhere,
plying in our right hands red swords
against the ardent multitudes of Echu Íuil.
There is no pride in me,
I am neither proud nor arrogant, woman.

'Do not be angry, then,' said Lí Ban, 'for Cú Chulaind's charioteer, Lóeg, is here with the message that Cú Chulaind will bring a host.' Labraid greeted the charioteer, saying, 'Welcome, Lóeg, for the sake of the woman with whom you have come and for the sake of everyone from whom you have come. Go home, now, and Lí Ban will follow you.'

Lóeg returned to Emuin, then, and related his adventure to Cú Chulaind and everyone else. Cú Chulaind sat up in bed and passed his hand over his face; then he spoke clearly to Lóeg, for the news the charioteer had brought had strengthened his spirits.

Cú Chulaind told Lóeg, 'Go now to Emer and say to her that women of the Síde* have come and destroyed me; tell her that I am mending and let her come and visit me.' But Lóeg recited this poem to strengthen Cú Chulaind:

> Great folly for a warrior
> to lie under the spell of a wasting sickness;
> it shows that spirits,
> the folk of Tenmag Trogagi,
> have bound you,
> and tortured you,
> and destroyed you,
> through the power of a wanton woman.
> Awake! Then the woman's mockery will shatter
> and your glorious valour will shine
> among champions and warriors;
> you will recover fully,

* Fairies, or spirits of the other-world.

and take to action
and perform glorious deeds.
When the call of Labraid sounds,
O warlike man, rise that you might be great.

Lóeg went then to Emer and told her of Cú Chulaind's condition. 'Bad luck to you,' she said, 'for you visited the Síde and brought back no cure for your lord. Shame on the Ulaid for not trying to heal him. If Conchubur were consumed, or Fergus overcome by sleep, or Conall Cernach laid low with wounds, Cú Chulaind would aid them.' And she recited this poem:

Alas, son of Ríangabur,
that you visited the Síde
and returned with no cure
for the son of Deichtine's spectre.

Shame on the Ulaid, with their generosity
among foster-fathers and foster-brothers,
not to be searching the dark world
to help their friend Cú Chulaind.

If Fergus had sunk into sleep,
and a single druid's art could heal,
the son of Deichtine would not rest
until that druid had made his examination.

Or if it were Conall
who was beset by wounds and injuries,
the Hound would search the wide world
until he found a doctor to heal him.

If Lóegure Búadach were faced
with an overwhelming danger,
Cú would search the meadows of Ériu
to cure the son of Connad son of Iliu.

If it were Celtchair of the deceits
to whom sleep and long wasting had come,
Sétantae would be journeying
night and day through the Síde.

If it were Furbude of the Fían
who was laid low for a long time,
Cú would search the hard earth
until he found a cure.

Dead the hosts of Síd Truim,
dispersed their great deeds;
since the sleep of the Síde seized him,
their Hound outstrips hounds no more.

Alas! Your sickness touches me,
Hound of the smith of Conchubur;
my heart and mind are troubled –
I wonder if I might heal him.

Alas! Blood my heart,
wasting for the horsemen of the plain
unless he should come here
from the assembly of Mag Muirthemni.

He comes not from Emuin –
a spectre has parted us.
My voice is weak and mute
because he is in an evil state.

A month and a season and a year
without sleeping together,
without hearing a man
of pleasing speech, son of Ríangabur.

After that Emer went to Emuin to visit Cú Chulaind; she sat on his bed and said, 'Shame on you, lying there for love of a woman – long lying will make you sick.' Then she recited this poem:

Rise, warrior of Ulaid!
Awake healthy and happy from sleep!
See the king of Emuin early in the morning –
do not indulge in excessive sleep.

See his shoulder full with crystal,
see his splendid drinking horns,
see his chariots traversing the valley,
see his ranks of fidchell pieces.

See the vigorous champions,
see his tall and gentle women,
see his kings – a course of danger –
see his very great queens.

See the onset of brilliant winter,
see each wonder in turn;
see then that which you serve,
its coldness and distance and dimness.

Heavy sleep wastes, is not good;
weariness follows oppression.
Long sleep is a draught added to satiety;
weakness is next to death.

Throw off sleep, the peace that follows drink,
throw it off with great energy.
Many gentle words have loved you.
Rise, warrior of Ulaid!

Cú Chulaind rose, then, and passed his hand over his face
and threw off all weariness and sluggishness; he rose and went
to Airbe Rofir. There he saw Lí Ban approaching; she spoke
to him and invited him to the Síde. 'Where does Labraid
dwell?' he asked. 'Not difficult, that,' she answered:

Labraid dwells on a clear lake
frequented by troops of women.
If you decide to meet him,
you will not regret your visit.

His bold right hand cuts down hundreds –
she who tells you knows.
Like the beautiful colour
of a violet his cheek.

Conchend keen for battle trembles
before the slender red sword of Labraid;
Labraid crushes the spears of foolish hosts
and breaks the shields of armoured warriors.

In combat his skin is as bright as his eyes.
More honourable than the men of the Síde,
he does not betray friends in great need.
He has cut down many thousands.

Greater his fame than that of young warriors:
he has invaded the land of Echu Íuil.
Like threads of gold his hair,
and his breath reeks of wine.

34

Most wonderful of men, he initiates battles;
fierce he is at distant borders.
Boats and horses race
past the island where Labraid dwells.

A man of many deeds across the sea:
Labraid Lúathlám ar Cladeb.
No fighting disturbs his domain –
the sleep of a multitude prevails.

Bridles of red gold for his horses,
and nothing but this:
pillars of silver and crystal.
That is the house where he dwells.

But Cú Chulaind replied, 'I will not go upon the invitation of a woman.' 'Then let Lóeg come and see everything,' said Lí Ban. Lóeg accompanied Lí Ban, then. They went to Mag Lúada and An Bile Búada, over Óenach nEmna and into Óenach Fidgai, and there they found Áed Abrat and his daughters. Fand greeted Lóeg, asking, 'Why has Cú Chulaind himself not come?' 'He would not come upon a woman's invitation, nor until he learned if it was from you that the invitation came.' 'It was from me,' said Fand. 'Now return to him at once, for the battle is today.'

Lóeg returned to Cú Chulaind, then, and Cú Chulaind asked him, 'How does it look, Lóeg?' Lóeg answered, 'Time it is to go, for the battle will be today.' Then he recited this poem:

I arrived to find splendid sport,
a wonderful place, though all was customary.
I came to a mound, to scores of companies,
among which I found long-haired Labraid.

I found him sitting
in the mound, with thousands of weapons;
beautiful yellow hair he had,
tied back with a gold apple.

He recognized me, then,
by my five-folded crimson cloak.
He said to me, 'Will you come with me
to the house of Failbe Find?'

Two kings there are in the house:
Failbe Find and Labraid;
a great throng in the one house:
three fifties of men for each king.

Fifty beds on the right side
and fifty on the floor;
fifty beds on the left side
and fifty on the dias.

Bedposts of bronze,
white gilded pillars;
the candle before them
a bright precious stone.

At the doorway to the west,
where the sun sets,
a herd of grey horses, bright their manes,
and a herd of chestnut horses.

At the doorway to the east,
three trees of brilliant crystal,
whence a gentle flock of birds calls
to the children of the royal fort.

A tree at the doorway to the court,
fair its harmony;
a tree of silver before the setting sun,
its brightness like that of gold.

Three score trees there
whose crowns are meetings that do not meet.
Each tree bears ripe fruit.
for three hundred men.

There is in the Síde a well
with three fifties of brightly coloured mantles,
a pin of radiant gold
in the corner of each mantle.

A vat of intoxicating mead
was being distributed to the household.
It is there yet, its state unchanging –
it is always full.

There is too in the house a woman
who would be distinguished among the women of Ériu:
she appears with yellow hair
and great beauty and charm.

Fair and wondrous
her conversation with everyone,
and the hearts of all men break
with love and affection for her.

This woman said, then,
'Who is that lad I do not recognize?
Come here for a while if it is you,
servant of the man of Muirthemne.'

I went very slowly,
fearing for my honour.
She said to me, 'Will he come to us,
the excellent only son of Deichtine?'

A pity that son did not go himself,
with everyone asking for him;
he could have seen for himself
the great house I visited.

If I possessed all of Ériu
and the kingship of yellow Brega,
I would give it all, no bad bargain,
to live in the place I visited.

'Good, that,' said Cú Chulaind. 'Good, indeed, and good
that you should go, for everything in that land is good,' said
Lóeg. And he spoke on about the delights of the Síde:

I saw a bright and noble land
where neither lie nor falsehood is spoken.
There lives a king who reddens troops:
Labraid Lúathlám ar Cladeb.

Passing across Mag Lúada,
I was shown An Bile Búada;
At Mag Denda I seized
a pair of two-headed snakes.

As we were together,
Lí Ban said to me,
'A dear miracle it would be
if you were Cú Chulaind and not you.'

A troop of beautiful women – victory without restraint –
the daughters of Áed Abrat,
but the beauty of Fand – brilliant sound –
neither king nor queen can match.

I could enumerate, as I know them,
the descendants of sinless Adam,
and still the beauty of Fand
would find no equal.

I saw gleaming warriors
slashing with their weapons;
I saw coloured garments,
garb that was not ignoble.

I saw gentle women feasting;
I saw their daughters.
I saw noble youths
traversing the wooded ridge.

I saw musicians in the house,
playing for the women;
but for the speed with which I left,
I would have been rendered helpless.

I have seen the hill where stood
the beautiful Eithne Ingubai,
but the woman I speak of now
would deprive troops of their senses.

Cú Chulaind went to this land, then; he took his chariot,
and they reached the island. Labraid welcomed him, and all
the women welcomed him, and Fand gave him a special
welcome. 'What now?' asked Cú Chulaind. Labraid answered,

'Not difficult, that – we will take a turn around the assembled host.' They went out and found the host and looked it over, and the enemy seemed innumerable. 'Go now,' Cú Chulaind said to Labraid, so Labraid left, but Cú Chulaind remained with the host. Two druidic ravens announced Cú Chulaind's presence; the host perceived this and said, 'No doubt the ravens are announcing the frenzied one of Ériu.' And the host hunted them down until there was for the birds no place in the land.

Early one morning, Echu Íuil went to wash his hands in a spring; Cú Chulaind spied the man's shoulder through an opening in his mantle and cast a spear through it. Thirty-three of the host were killed by Cú Chulaind. Finally, Senach Síaborthe attacked, and they fought a great battle before Cú Chulaind killed him. Labraid came, then, and routed the entire host; he asked Cú Chulaind to desist from the slaughter, but Lóeg said, 'I fear that the man will turn his anger against us, for he has not yet had his fill of fighting. Have three vats of cold water brought, that his rage might be extinguished.' The first vat that Cú Chulaind entered boiled over, and the second became so hot that no one could endure it, but the third grew only moderately warm.

When the women saw Cú Chulaind, Fand recited this poem:

> Stately the chariot-warrior who travels the road,
> though he be young and beardless;
> fair the driver who crosses the plain,
> at evening, to Óenach Fidgai.

The song he sings is not the music of the Síde:
it is the stain of blood that is on him;
the wheels of his chariot echo
the bass song that he sings.

May the horses under his smooth chariot
stay for me a little, that I may look at them;
as a team their like is not to be found –
they are as swift as a wind of spring.

Fifty gold apples play overhead,
performing tricks on his breath;
as a king his like is not to be found,
not among gentle, not among fierce.

In each of his cheeks
a spot red as blood,
a green spot, a blue spot
and a spot of pale purple.

Seven lights in his eye –
he is not one to be left sightless.
It has the ornament of a noble eye:
a dark, blue-black eyelash.

A man known throughout Ériu
is already good; and this one has
hair of three different colours,
this young beardless lad,

A red sword that blood reddens
right up to its hilt of silver;
a shield with a boss of yellow gold
and a rim of white metal.

He steps over men in every battle;
valorous he enters the place of danger.
None of your fierce warriors
can match Cú Chulaind.

The warrior from Muirthemne,
Cú Chulaind, came here;
the daughters of Áed Abrat
they who brought him.

A long red drop of blood,
a fury rising to the treetops,
a proud high shout of victory,
a wailing that scatters spectres.

Lí Ban greeted him, then, with this poem:

Welcome, Cú Chulaind,
advancing boar,
great chieftain of Mag Muirthemni.
Great his spirit,
honour of battle-victorious champions,
heart of heroes,
strong stone of wisdom,
red in anger,
ready for the fair play of enemies,
one of the valorous warriors of Ulaid.
Beautiful his brilliance,
bright of eye to women.
Welcome, Cú Chulaind!

'What have you done, Cú Chulaind?' Lí Ban asked. Cú Chulaind answered:

I have cast my spear
into the camp of Éogan Indber;
I do not know, famous its path,
whether my shot hit or missed.

Whether better or worse for my strength,
I have never yet in fair play
cast ignorantly at a man in the mist –
perhaps not a soul is left alive.

A fair shining host with splendid horses
pursued me from every direction:
the people of Manandán son of Ler
whom Éogan Indber summoned.

Whichever way I turned
when my full fury came upon me,
it was one man against three thousand,
and I sent them towards death.

I heard Echu Íuil groan,
a sound that came from the heart;
if that truly was one man, and not an army,
then my cast was well aimed.

Cú Chulaind slept with Fand, then, and he stayed with her
for a month. When he bade her farewell, she said to him,
'Where will we meet?' They decided upon Ibor Cind Tráchta.
This was told to Emer, and she prepared knives with which to
kill Fand. Fifty women accompanied Emer to the place of the
meeting. Cú Chulaind and Lóeg were playing fidchell and did
not notice the advancing women, but Fand noticed, and she
said to Lóeg, 'Look over at what I am seeing.' 'What is
it?' asked Lóeg, and he looked.

Fand then said, 'Lóeg, look behind you. Listening to you is a troop of clever, capable women, glittering sharp knives in their right hands and gold on their breasts. When warriors go to their battle chariots, a fair form will be seen: Emer daughter of Forgall in a new guise.'

'Have no fear,' replied Cú Chulaind, 'for she will not come at all. Step up into my powerful chariot, with its sunny seat, and I will protect you from every woman in the four quarters of Ériu, for though the daughter of Forgall may boast to her companions about her mighty deeds, she is not likely to challenge me.' He said to Emer, then, 'I avoid you, woman, as every man avoids the one he loves. I will not strike your hard spear, held with trembling hand; neither do you threaten me with your thin, feeble knife and weak, restrained anger, for the strength of women is insufficient to demand my full power.'

'Why, then, Cú Chulaind, have you dishonoured me before the people of the province and the women of Ériu and all people of rank?' asked Emer. 'It is under your protection I have come, under the great power of your guarantee; and though the pride of mighty conflicts makes you boastful, perhaps your attempt to leave me will fail, lad, however much you try.'

'Emer, why will you not permit me to meet this woman?' replied Cú Chulaind. 'She is pure and modest, fair and clever and worthy of a king. A handsome sight she is on the waves of the great-tided sea, with her shapeliness and beauty and noble family, her embroidery and handiwork, her good sense and prudence and steadfastness, her abundance of horses and herds of cattle. Whatever you may promise, there is nothing under heaven her husband could desire that she would not do. Neither will you find a handsome, combat-scarred, battle-victorious champion to equal me.'

'Perhaps this woman you have chosen is no better than I,' answered Emer. 'But what's red is beautiful, what's new is bright, what's tall is fair, what's familiar is stale. The unknown is honoured, the known is neglected – until all is known. Lad, we lived togther in harmony once, and we could do so again if only I still pleased you.'

Cú Chulaind grew melancholy at this, and he said, 'By my word, you do please me, and you will as long as you live.' 'Leave me, then,' said Fand. 'Better to leave me,' said Emer. 'No, I should be left,' said Fand, 'for it is I who was threatened just now.' And she began to cry and grieve, for being abandoned was shameful to her; she went to her house, and the great love she bore Cú Chulaind troubled her, and she recited this poem:

> I will continue my journey
> though I prefer my great adventure here;
> whoever might come, great his fame,
> I would prefer to remain with Cú Chulaind.
>
> I would prefer to remain here –
> that I grant willingly –
> than to go, it may surprise you to learn,
> to the sun-house of Áed Abrat.
>
> Emer, the man is yours,
> and may you enjoy him, good woman.
> What my hand cannot obtain
> I must still desire.

Many a man has sought me,
both openly and in secret;
yet I never went to meet them,
for I was upright.

Wretched she who gives her love
if he takes no notice of her;
better to put such thoughts aside
unless she is loved as she loves.

Fifty women came here,
Emer of the yellow hair,
to fall upon Fand – a bad idea –
and kill her in her misery.

But I have three fifties of women,
beautiful and unmarried, at home
with me in my fort –
they would not desert me.

When Manandán learned that Fand was in danger from the
women of Ulaid and that she was being forsaken by Cú
Chulaind, he came west after her and stood before her, and no
one but Fand could see him. When she perceived him, Fand
felt deep regret and sadness, and she recited this poem:

See the warlike son of Ler
on the plains of Éogan Indber:
Manandán, lord of the world –
once I held him dear.

Then, I would have wept,
but my proud spirit does not love now –
love is a vain thing
that goes about heedlessly and foolishly.

When Manandán and I lived
in the sun-house at Dún Indber,
we both thought it likely
we would never separate.

When fair Manandán married me,
I was a proper wife:
he never won from me
the odd game of fidchell.

When fair Manandán married me,
I was a proper wife:
a bracelet of gold he gave me,
the price of making me blush.

Outside on the heath I had
fifty beautiful women;
I gave him fifty men
in addition to the fifty women.

Two hundred, and no mistake,
the people of our house:
one hundred strong, healthy men,
one hundred fair, thriving women.

Across the ocean I see
(and he who does not is a fool)
the horsemen of the foaming sea,
he who does not follow the long ships.

Your going past us now
none but the Síde might perceive;
your keen sight magnifies the tiniest host,
though it be far and distant.

That keen sight would be useful to me,
for the senses of women are foolish:
the one whom I loved so completely
has put me in danger here.

Farewell to you, dear Cú!
I leave you with head held high.
I wish that I were not going –
every rule is good until broken.

Time for me is set out, now –
there is someone who finds that difficult.
My distress is great,
O Lóeg, O son of Ríangabur.

I will go with my own husband, now
for he will not deny me.
Lest you say I left in secret,
look now, if you wish.

Fand set out after Manandán, then, and he greeted her and said, 'Well, woman, are you waiting for Cú Chulaind or will you go with me?' 'By my word, there is a man I would prefer as husband. But it is with you I will go; I will not wait for Cú Chulaind, for he has betrayed me. Another thing, good person, you have no other worthy queen, but Cú Chulaind does.'

When Cú Chulaind perceived that Fand was leaving with Manandán, he asked Lóeg, 'What is this?' 'Not difficult, that – Fand is going away with Manandán son of Ler, for she did not please you.' At that, Cú Chulaind made three high leaps and three southerly leaps, toward Lúachair; he was a long time in the mountains without food or water, sleeping each night on Slige Midlúachra.

Emer went to Conchubur in Emuin and told him of Cú Chulaind's state and Conchubur ordered the poets and artisans and druids of Ulaid to find Cú Chulaind and secure him and bring him back. Cú Chulaind tried to kill the artisans, but the druids sang spells over him until his hands and feet were bound and he came to his senses. He asked for a drink; the druids brought a drink of forgetfulness, and, when he drank that, he forgot Fand and everything he had done. Since Emer was no better off, they brought her a drink that she might forget her jealousy. Moreover, Manandán shook his cloak between Cú Chulaind and Fand, that they might never meet again.

Bricriu's Feast

Bricriu Nemthenga prepared a great feast for Conchubur son of Ness and all of Ulaid. He spent an entire year preparing this feast: he had an ornamented mansion built for the guests, and he had it erected at Dún Rudrige. Bricriu's house was built in the likeness of the Cráebrúad at Emuin Machae, but this house surpassed the Cráebrúad as to materials and workmanship, beauty and decoration, pillars and façades, carvings and lintels, radiance and beauty, comeliness and excellence – in short, it surpassed every house of that time. It was constructed on the plan of the Tech Midchúarta: there were nine apartments between the hearth and the wall, and each façade was thirty feet high and made of bronze, and there was gold ornamentation everywhere. A royal apartment for Conchubur was erected at the front of the royal house, high above the other couches, and it was ornamented with carbuncle and other precious things; it shone with the radiance of gold and silver and carbuncle and every colour, so that it was as bright by night as by day. Round this apartment were built twelve apartments, for the twelve warriors of Ulaid. The workmanship of this house was as good as the materials used to build it: a team of oxen was required to draw each pillar, and seven of the strongest men of Ulaid to fix each pillar; and thirty of the chief seers of Ériu came to place and arrange everything.

Bricriu also had built, for himself, a bower, and it was as high as Conchubur's apartment and those of his warriors.

This bower was decorated with marvellous embroideries and hangings, and glass windows were set in on every side. And one of these windows was set over Bricriu's couch, in order that he might see what was going on, for he knew that the Ulaid would not allow him inside the house.

When all was ready – the great house, and the bower, and their provisioning with plaids and coverlets and quilts and pillows and food and drink – and when nothing was wanting as to furnishings and materials for the feast, Bricriu went off to Emuin Machae to see Conchubur and the chieftains of Ulaid. The Ulaid were holding a fair at Emuin that day; Bricriu was welcomed and placed at Conchubur's shoulder, and he said to Conchubur and to the chieftains, 'Come and enjoy my feast with me.' 'I am willing if the Ulaid are,' Conchubur answered, but Fergus son of Roech and the other chieftains said, 'We will not go. If we go to his feast, he will incite us against each other, and our dead will outnumber the living.' 'I will do worse than that if you do not come,' said Bricriu. 'What will you do?' asked Conchubur. 'I will incite the kings and the chiefs and the warriors and the young warriors,' said Bricriu, 'so that you will all kill one other unless you come to drink at my feast.' 'We will not go to avoid that,' said Conchubur. 'Then I will set son against father and incite them to kill each other,' said Bricriu. 'If that is not enough, I will set daughter against mother. And if that is not enough, I will incite the two breasts of every Ulaid woman to beat against each other and become foul and putrid.' 'In that case, it would be better to go,' said Fergus. 'Let a few chieftains form a council, if that seems right,' said Senchae son of Ailill, and Conchubur agreed, saying, 'Evil will come of our not adopting some plan.'

The chieftains formed a council, then, and, as they discussed the matter, Senchae gave the following advice: 'Since you must go with Bricriu, require him to give hostages, and as soon as he has set out the feast, send eight swordsmen to escort him from the house.' Furbude son of Conchubur took that decision to Bricriu, and Bricriu replied, 'I will be happy to abide by that.' Thus the Ulaid set out from Emuin Machae, each band with its king, each troop with its leader, each host with its chieftain – a marvellously handsome procession it was, with the warriors and the men of might making for the royal house.

Bricriu, meanwhile, began to think how he might incite the Ulaid once he had given them their hostages; and when he had given the matter considerable thought, he went to Lóegure Búadach son of Connad son of Iliu. 'Well met, Lóegure Búadach,' he said, 'mighty blow of Brega, seething blow of Mide, bearer of red flame, victor over the youth of Ulaid! Why should you not always have the champion's portion at Emuin?' 'Indeed, it is mine if I want it,' said Lóegure. 'I will make you king over all the warriors of Ériu if you follow my advice,' said Bricriu. 'Then I will follow it,' said Lóegure. 'Once the champion's portion is yours at my house,' Bricriu continued, 'it will be yours at Emuin for ever. And the champion's portion at my house will be worth contesting, for it is not the portion of a fool. I have a cauldron that would hold three of the warriors of Ulaid, and it has been filled with undiluted wine. I have a seven-year-old boar that since it was a piglet has eaten nothing but gruel and meal and fresh milk in spring, curds and sweet milk in summer, nuts and wheat in autumn and meat and broth in winter. I have a lordly cow that is also seven years old, and, since it was a calf, it has eaten nothing but heather and twigs and fresh milk and herbs and meadow grass and corn. I have one hundred wheat cakes cooked in honey; twenty-five bushels of wheat were brought for these cakes, so that each bushel made just four cakes. That is what the champion's portion is like at my house. Since you are the best warrior in Ulaid, it is yours by right, and I intend that you should have it. Once the feast has been set out, at the end of the day, have your charioteer rise, and the champion's portion will be given to him.' 'Indeed, it will,' said Lóegure, 'or blood will flow.' Bricriu laughed at that and was content.

When he had finished with Lóegure Búadach, Bricriu went to the host of Conall Cernach. 'Well met, Conall,' he began, 'for you are a warrior of combats and victories – already you have earned great triumphs over the youths of Ulaid. When the Ulaid venture out to the borders of enemy lands, you are three days and three nights ahead of them in crossing fords; and, when they return, you protect their rear – no enemy slips past them or through them or round them. Is there any reason you should not have the champion's portion at Emuin Machae for ever?' If Bricriu was treacherous in dealings with Lóegure, he was twice as deceitful when he spoke with Conall. And after he had induced Conall to agree with him, he went to the host of Cú Chulaind. 'Well met, Cú Chulaind,' he began, 'battle victor of Brega, bright flag of the Life, darling of Emuin, sweetheart of the women and the young girls. Today, Cú Chulaind is no nickname, for you are the great boaster of Ulaid. You defend us from great onslaughts and attacks, you seek the rights to everyone in Ulaid, and where everyone else attempts, you succeed. All Ériu acknowledges your bravery and valour and high deeds. Why, then, should you leave the champion's portion to anyone else in Ulaid when there is not a man in Ériu capable of meeting you in combat?' 'Indeed! I swear by what my people swear by,' said Cú Chulaind, 'the man who comes to fight me will be a man without a head!' After that, Bricriu left the three heroes and mingled with the hosts as if he had done no mischief at all.

The Ulaid arrived at Bricriu's house, and each man settled into his apartment in the royal dwelling, king and prince and chieftain and young lord and young warrior. On one side of the house, the heroes of Ulaid gathered round Conchubur, while, on the other side, the women of Ulaid assembled round Conchubur's wife, Mugain daughter of Echu Feidlech. The heroes who gathered round Conchubur in the front of the house included Fergus son of Roech, Celtchair son of Uthechar, Éogan son of Durthacht, the king's two sons Fíachu and Fíachach, Fergnae son of Findchóem, Fergus son of Léti, Cúscraid Mend son of Conchubur, Senchae son of Ailill, Fíachu's three sons Rus and Dáre and Imchad, Muinremur son of Gerrgend, Errge Echbél, Amorgen son of Ecet, Mend son of Salchad, Dubthach Dóeltenga, Feradach Find Fechtnach, Fedilmid Chilair Chétach, Furbude Fer Bend, Rochad son of Fathemon, Lóegure Búadach, Conall Cernach, Cú Chulaind, Connad son of Mornae, Erc son of Fedilmid, Illand son of Fergus, Findtan son of Níall, Cethernd son of Findtan, Fachtna son of Senchad, Condlae Sáeb, Ailill Miltenga, Bricriu himself and the choicest warriors of Ulaid, together with the youths and the entertainers.

The musicians and the players performed while the feast

was being set out, and when everything was in place, Bricriu was ordered to leave the house, as a consequence of the hostages he had given. The hostages rose, naked swords in hand, to expel Bricriu from the house, and so he left, with his household, and repaired to the bower. But, as he was about to leave the royal house, he said to the gathering, 'Yonder you see the champion's portion, and it is no portion from the house of a fool; therefore, let it be given to the best warrior in Ulaid.' With that, he left.

Thereupon, the servers rose to do their work, and there rose also the charioteer of Lóegure Búadach, Sedlang son of Ríangabur, and he said to the distributors, 'Bring that champion's portion over here, to Lóegure Búadach, for he is the most deserving of it in Ulaid.' Id son of Ríangabur, Conall Cernach's charioteer, rose and said the same about Conall. And Lóeg son of Ríangabur, Cú Chulaind's charioteer, said to the distributors, 'Bring the champion's portion to Cú Chulaind – no shame for the Ulaid to give it to him, for he is the most accomplished warrior here.' 'Not true, that,' said Lóegure Búadach and Conall Cernach, and, at that, the three heroes rose out into the middle of the house with their spears and swords and shields; and they so slashed at each other that half the house was a fire of swords and glittering spear edges, while the other half was a pure-white bird flock of shield enamel. A great alarm went up in the royal house, and the valiant warriors of Ulaid trembled; Conchubur and Fergus son of Roech were furious at seeing the unfair and unconscionable attack of two against one, Lóegure and Conall attacking Cú Chulaind. Not a man of the Ulaid dared separate them, however, until Senchae said to Conchubur, 'Part the men', for

Senchae was the earthly god among the Ulaid in the time of Conchubur.

Conchubur and Fergus stepped between the combatants, then, and the men at once dropped their hands to their sides. 'Let my will prevail,' said Senchae. 'We agree,' said the men. 'It is my will,' said Senchae, 'that the champion's portion be divided among the host tonight and that tomorrow the dispute be submitted to Ailill son of Mágu, since it is bad luck for the Ulaid to settle an argument without a judgement from Crúachu.' The food and drink were shared out, then, and everyone formed a circle round the fire, and the assembly grew drunken and merry.

Bricriu, meanwhile, was in his bower with his queen, and he could see from his couch how matters stood in the royal house. He pondered how he might incite the women as he had incited the men, and, just as he finished his meditation, Fedelm Noíchride and her fifty women emerged from the royal house after some heavy drinking. Bricriu perceived her going past and said, 'Well met tonight, wife of Lóegure Búadach! Fedelm Noíchride is not just a nickname, not considering your form and your intelligence and your lineage. Conchubur, a provincial king of Ériu, is your father, Lóegure Búadach is your husband, and it would hardly be to your honour if any woman of Ulaid were to precede you into the Tech Midchúarta – rather, the women of all Ulaid should follow upon your heel. If you enter the house first tonight, you will always be first among the women of Ulaid.' Thereupon Fedelm went out to the third ridge from the house.

After that, Lendabair, the daughter of Éogan son of Durthacht and the wife of Conall Cernach, came out. Bricriu accosted her and said, 'Well met, Lendabair! No nickname yours, for you are the centre of attention and the sweetheart of the men of all the world, and that by reason of your beauty and your fame. As your husband outdoes the men of the world in weaponry and in appearance, so you outdo the women of Ulaid.' As deceitful as he had been in talking to Fedelm, he was twice as deceitful in dealing with Lendabair.

After that, Emer came out with her fifty women, and Bricriu greeted her, saying, 'Your health, Emer, daughter of Forgall Manach and wife of the best man in Ériu. Emer Foltchaín is no nickname, either, for the kings and princes of Ériu glitter round you. As the sun outshines the stars of the sky, so you outshine the women of the entire world, and that by reason of your shape and form and lineage, your youth and beauty and fame and your intelligence and discernment and eloquence.' Although he had been very deceitful in dealing with the other two women, Bricriu was thrice as deceitful in dealing with Emer.

All three companies of women went out to the same spot, the third ridge from the house, and no wife knew that the other two had been incited by Bricriu. And all three women set out for the house. At the first ridge, the procession was steady and stately and measured – one foot was scarcely lifted above the other. At the second ridge, however, the steps became shorter and quicker. By the third ridge, the women were striving to keep up with each other, and they all raised their skirts to their hips, for Bricriu had told each woman that she who entered the house first would be queen over the entire province. The tumult that arose from their striving was like the tumult from the arrival of fifty chariots; it so shook the house that the warriors inside sprang for their weapons and tried to kill each other. But Senchae said, 'Wait! This is not the arrival of enemies – rather, Bricriu has incited the women outside to strife. I swear by what my people swear by, if he is not expelled from this house, the dead will outnumber the living.' At that, the doorkeepers closed the door. Emer daughter of Forgall Manach reached the door first, by reason of her speed, and she put her back against the door and entreated the doorkeepers to open it before the other women arrived. Thereupon the men inside rose, each meaning to open the door for his own wife so that she might be the first to enter. 'An evil night,' said Conchubur, and he struck the silver sceptre in his hand against the bronze pillar of his couch, and the host sat down. Senchae said, 'Wait! Not a war of weapons this, but a war of words.'

With that, each woman drew back from the door, under the protection of her husband, and there began a war of words among the women of Ulaid. Upon hearing the praises of their wives, Lóegure and Conall sprang up into the warrior's moon; each of them broke off a pole as tall as himself from the house, and that way Fedelm and Lendabair were able to enter. Cú Chulaind, however, lifted the side of the house opposite his apartment so high that the stars were visible beneath the wall; Emer was thus able to enter with her fifty women and the fifty women of each of the other two wives. He then set the house back down; seven feet of panelling sank into the ground, and the fort shook so much that Bricriu's bower fell, and Bricriu and his wife were thrown on to the garbage heap in the courtyard, among the dogs.

'Alas! Enemies are attacking the fort,' said Bricriu, and he rose quickly and looked at his house, and it seemed to have been destroyed, for one side had fallen down. He beat on the door, then, and the Ulaid let him in, for he was so besmirched that they did not recognize him until he began to speak. He stood in the middle of the house and said, 'Unlucky this feast that I have prepared for you, men of Ulaid. My house is dearer to me than all my possessions, and there is a geiss against your eating or sleeping until you leave it just as you found it when you arrived.'

Thereupon all the warriors of Ulaid rose and tried to restore the house, but they could not even raise it high enough for the wind to pass underneath. This was a problem for the Ulaid. Senchae said, 'I can only advise you to ask the man who made the house lopsided to set it straight.' The Ulaid then asked Cú Chulaind to put the house to rights, and Bricriu said, 'King of the warriors of Ériu, if you cannot restore the house, no one in the world can.' All the Ulaid entreated Cú Chulaind to help them, and he rose up so that the feasters would not have to go without food and drink. He attempted to straighten the house, and he failed. Then his ríastarthae came over him: a drop of blood appeared at the tip of each hair, and he drew his hair into his head, so that, from above, his jet-black locks appeared to have been cropped with scissors; he turned like a mill wheel, and he stretched himself out until a warrior's foot could fit between each pair of ribs. His power and energy returned to him, and he lifted the house and reset it so that it was straight as it had been before.

After that, they had a pleasant time enjoying the feast. On one side of the illustrious Conchubur, the golden high king of Ulaid, gathered the kings and chiefs, and on the other side were the queens: Mugain Attencháithrech daughter of Echu Feidlech and wife of Conchubur son of Ness, Fedelm Noíchride daughter of Conchubur (nine forms she displayed, and each was lovelier than the last), Fedelm Foltchaín (Conchubur's other daughter and the wife of Lóegure Búadach), Findbec daughter of Echu and wife of Cethernd son of Findtan, Brig Brethach wife of Celtchair son of Uthechar, Findige daughter of Echu and wife of Éogan son of Durthacht, Findchóem daughter of Cathub and wife of Amorgen Íarngiunnach, Derborcaill wife of Lugaid Réoderg son of the three Finds of Emuin, Emer Foltchaín daughter of Forgall Manach and wife of Cú Chulaind son of Súaltaim, Lendabair daughter of Éogan son of Durthacht and wife of Conall Cernach, and Níam daughter of Celtchair son of Uthechar and wife of Cormac Cond Longes son of Conchubur. There was no counting the number of beautiful women at that feast.

And yet the women began once again to squabble over their men and themselves, with the result that the three heroes all but resumed their combat. Senchae son of Ailill rose and shook his staff, and the men of Ulaid fell silent. He spoke words to chasten the women, but Emer continued to praise her husband. Thereupon Conall Cernach said, 'Woman, if your words are true, let the lad of feats come here, that I might oppose him.' 'Not at all,' said Cú Chulaind, 'for I am tired and broken to pieces. Today, I will eat and sleep, but I will not undertake combat.' All this was in fact true, by reason of Cú Chulaind's encounter that day with the Líath Machae by the shore of Lind Léith near Slíab Fúait. The horse had come towards him from the lake, Cú Chulaind had put his arms round its neck, and the two of them had circled all

Ériu until at last night fell and the horse was broken. (Cú Chulaind found the Dub Sainglend in the same way, at Loch Duib Sainglaind.) Cú Chulaind went on: 'Today the Líath Machae and I have sought out the great hostels of Ériu: Brega, Mide, Muresc, Muirthemne, Macha, Mag Medba, Currech, Cletech, Cernae, Lía, Líne, Locharna, Fea, Femen, Fergna, Urros, Domnand, Ros Roigne, Anni Éo. Better every feat of sleeping, dearer food than anything else. I swear by the god my people swear by, if I had my fill of food and sleep, there would be no trick or feat that any man could meet me at.'

It happened, thus, that the dispute over the champion's portion arose again. Conchubur and the chieftains of Ulaid intervened to pronounce judgement, and Conchubur said, 'Go now to the man who will undertake to decide this matter, Cú Rui son of Dáre.' 'I will agree to that,' said Cú Chulaind. 'So will I,' said Lóegure. 'Let us go, then,' said Conall Cernach. 'Let horses be brought and yoked to Conall's chariot,' said Cú Chulaind. 'Alas!' said Conall. 'Indeed,' replied Cú Chulaind, 'for everyone knows well the clumsiness of your horses and the slowness of your gait and bearing and the great ponderousness with which your chariot moves; each wheel digs a ditch, so that everywhere you leave a track that is visible to the Ulaid for a year.' 'Do you hear that, Lóegure?' Conall asked. 'Indeed – but it is not I who have been disgraced and embarrassed. I am quick to cross fords – many fords – and I breast storms of many spears in front of the youths of Ulaid. I will not grant the superiority of kings until I have practised my chariot feats before kings and heroes in single chariots, over difficult and treacherous terrain, in wooded places and along

61

enemy borders, in order that no single-charioted hero might dare to meet me.'

With that, they yoked Lóegure's chariot, and he sprang into it; he drove across Mag Dá Gabul and Barrnaid na Forare and Áth Carpait Fergussa and Áth na Mórrigna to Cáerthend Clúana Dá Dam and into Clithar Fidbude, into Commur Cetharsliged, past Dún Delga, across Mag Slicech and west towards Slíab Breg. There, a great mist fell, thick and dark and impenetrable, so that he could not see his way. 'Let us stay here until the fog lifts,' he said to his charioteer, and he leapt down from his chariot. His charioteer was putting the horses out in a nearby meadow when he saw a giant man coming towards him, not a handsome fellow, either, but broad-shouldered, fat-mouthed, puffy-eyed, short-toothed, horribly wrinkled, beetle-browed, horrible and angry, strong, violent, ruthless, arrogant, destructive, snorting, big-sinewed, strong-forearmed, brave, rough and rustic. Cropped black hair he had, and a dun garment on him, and his rump swelled out under his tunic; there were filthy old shoes on his feet, and on his back he carried a great, heavy club, the size of a mill shaft. 'Whose horses are these, boy?' he asked, looking fierce. 'The horses of Lóegure Búadach, these,' answered the lad. 'True,' said the giant, 'and it is a good man whose horses these are.' As he said this, he took his club and gave the lad a blow from head to toe. At that, Lóegure came and said, 'Why did you strike my charioteer?' 'As punishment for trespassing in my meadow,' replied the giant. 'I will meet you myself,' said Lóegure, and they fought until Lóegure fled back to Emuin, leaving his horses and his charioteer and his weapons behind.

Not so long afterwards, Conall Cernach took the same route and arrived at the same plain where the druidic mist had fallen upon Lóegure. The same thick, dark, heavy clouds confronted Conall, so that he could see neither the sky nor the ground. He leapt down, then, and his charioteer turned the horses out into the same meadow, and soon they saw the giant coming towards them. The giant asked the lad who his master was, and the lad answered, 'Conall Cernach.' 'A good man, he,' said the giant, and he raised his club and gave the lad a blow from head to toe. The lad cried out, and Conall came running; Conall and the giant wrestled, but the latter had the stronger hold, so Conall fled, just as Lóegure had done, leaving behind his horses and his charioteer and his weapons.

After that, Cú Chulaind took the same route and arrived at the plain where the dark mist fell, just as before; he leapt down, Lóeg turned the horses out into the meadow. Soon Lóeg saw the giant coming towards him and asking him who his master was, and he answered, 'Cú Chulaind.' 'A good man, he,' said the giant, and he struck Lóeg with his club. Lóeg cried out, and Cú Chulaind came and wrestled with the giant; they pounded away at each other until the giant was worsted and forfeited his horses and chariot. Cú Chulaind took these, and his opponent's weapons, and bore them back to Emuin Machae in great triumph, presenting them as evidence of his victory.

'Yours is the champion's portion,' Bricriu then said to Cú Chulaind, 'for it is clear that no one else's deeds deserve comparison with yours.' But Lóegure and Conall said, 'Not true, Bricriu. We know that it was one of his friends from the Síde who came to play tricks on us and do us out of the champion's portion. We will not acknowledge his superiority on that account.' Conchubur and Fergus and the Ulaid failed to resolve the dispute, so they decided to seek out either Cú Rui son of Dáre or Ailill and Medb at Crúachu. The Ulaid assembled in council to discuss the pride and haughtiness of the three champions, and their decision was that the three should go to the house of Ailill son of Mágu and Medb in Crúachu for a judgement as to the champion's portion and the dispute of the women.

Handsome and graceful and effortless the procession of the Ulaid to Crúachu; Cú Chulaind, however, lagged behind the host, for he was entertaining the women of Ulaid with his feats of nine apples and nine javelins and nine knives, no one feat interfering with either of the others. His charioteer, Lóeg son of Ríangabur, went to where he was performing these feats and said, 'Pitiful wretch, your valour and your weaponry have disappeared, and the champion's portion has gone with it, for the Ulaid have long since reached Crúachu.' 'I had not noticed that, Lóeg. Yoke up the chariot, then,' said Cú Chulaind. By that time, the rest of the Ulaid had already reached Mag mBreg, but, after being scolded by his charioteer, Cú Chulaind travelled with such speed that the Líath Machae and the Dub Sainglend drew his chariot from Dún Rudrige across the length of Conchubur's province, across Slíab Fúait and Mag mBreg, and reached Crúachu before either Lóegure or Conall.

By reason of the speed and noise with which Conchubur and the warriors and chieftains of Ulaid reached Crúachu, the latter was badly shaken; weapons fell from their racks on the walls, and the host in the stronghold trembled like rushes in a river. Thereupon Medb said, 'Since the day I took possession of Crúachu, I have never heard thunder from a clear sky.' Findabair, the daughter of Ailill and Medb, went up to the balcony over the outer door of the fort, and she said, 'I see a chariot on the plain, dear mother.' 'Describe it,' said Medb, 'its form and appearance and equipment, the shape of its men, the colour of its horses and the manner of its arrival.' 'I see a chariot with two horses,' said Findabair, 'and they are furious, dapple grey, identical in form and colour and excellence and triumph and speed and leaping, sharp-eared, high-headed, high-spirited, wild, sinuous, narrow-nostrilled, flowing-maned, broad-chested, spotted all over, narrow-girthed, broad-backed, aggressive and with curly manes and tails. The chariot is of spruce and wicker, with black, smooth-turning wheels and beautifully woven reins; it has hard, blade-straight poles, a glistening new body, a curved yoke of pure silver, and pure yellow braided reins. The man has long, braided yellow hair with three colours on it: dark brown at the base, blood red in the middle and golden yellow at the tip. Three circlets on his head, each in its proper place next to the others. A fair scarlet tunic round him and embroidered with gold and silver; a speckled shield with a border of white gold in his hand; a barbed, five-pointed spike in his red-flaming fist. A flock of wild birds above the frame of his chariot.'

'We recognize that man by his description,' said Medb. 'I swear by what my people swear by, if it is in anger and rage that Lóegure Búadach comes to us, his sharp blade will cut us to the ground like leeks; a nice slaughter he will bring upon the host here at Crúachu unless his strength and ardour and fury are heeded and his anger is diminished.'

'I see another chariot on the plain, dear mother,' said Findabair, 'and it looks no worse.' 'Describe it,' said Medb. 'I see one pair of horses,' Findabair said, 'white-faced, copper-coloured, hardy, swift, fiery, bounding, broad-hooved, broad-chested, taking strong victorious strides across fords and estuaries and difficulties and winding roads and plains and glens, frenzied after a drunken victory like a bird in flight; my noble eye cannot describe the step by which it careers on its jealous course. The other horse is red, with a firmly braided mane, a broad back and forehead and a narrow girth; it is fierce, intense, strong and vicious, coursing over wide plains and rough and heavy terrain; it finds no difficulty in wooded land. The chariot is of spruce and wicker with wheels of white bronze, poles of pure silver, a noble, creaking frame, a haughty, curved yoke and reins with pure yellow fringes. The man has long, braided, beautiful hair; his face is half red and half white and bright and glistening all over. His cloak is blue and dark crimson. In one hand, a dark shield with a yellow boss and an edge of serrated bronze; in the other, which burns red, a red-burning spear. A flock of wild birds above the frame of his dusky chariot.'

'We recognize that man by his description,' said Medb. 'I swear by what my people swear by, we will be sliced up the way speckled fish are sliced by iron flails against bright-red stones – those are the small pieces Conall Cernach will cut us into if he is raging.'

'I see yet another chariot on the plain,' said Findabair. 'Describe it,' said Medb. 'One horse,' said Findabair, 'is grey, broad-thighed, fierce, swift, flying, ferocious, war-leaping, long-maned, noisy and thundering, curly-maned, high-headed, broad-chested; there shine the huge clods of earth that it cuts up with its very hard hooves. Its victorious stride overtakes flocks of birds; a dreadful flash its breath, a ball of flaming red fire, and the jaws of its bridle-bitted head shine. The other horse is jet black, hard-headed, compact, narrow-hooved, narrow-chested, strong, swift, arrogant, braided-maned, broad-backed, strong-thighed, high-spirited, fleet, fierce, long-striding, stout-blow-dealing, long-maned, long-tailed, swift at running after fighting, driving round paths and runs, scattering wastes, traversing glens and plains. The chariot is of spruce and wicker with iron wheels of rust yellow, poles of white gold, a bright, arching body of copper, and a curved yoke of pure gold and two braided reins of pure yellow. The sad, dark man in the chariot is the most beautiful man in Ériu. He wears a beautiful scarlet tunic, and over his white breast the opening is fastened by a brooch ornamented with gold, and his chest heaves violently. Eight dragon-red gems in his two eyes. His bright-shining, blood-red cheeks emit vapours and missiles of flame. Above his chariot he performs the hero's salmon leap, a feat for nine men.'

'A drop before the storm, that,' said Medb. 'We recognize that man by his description. I swear by what my people swear by, if it is in anger that Cú Chulaind comes to us, we will be ground into the earth and gravel the way a mill stone grinds very hard malt – even with the men of the entire province gathered round us in our defence – unless his anger and fury are diminished.'

Medb then went to the outer door of the courtyard, and she took with her three fifties of women and three vats of cold water with which to cool the ardour of the three heroes who were advancing before the host. The heroes were offered one house each or one house for the three of them. 'A house for each of us,' Cú Chulaind said, so magnificent bedding was brought into the houses, and the heroes were given their choice of the three fifties of girls, but Findabair was taken by Cú Chulaind into his own house.

The rest of the Ulaid arrived later; Ailill and Medb and their entire household went to greet the visitors, and Senchae son of Ailill replied, 'We are content.' The Ulaid entered the fort, then, the royal house was given over to them. There were façades of bronze and partitions of red yew, and three strips of bronze in the vault of the roof. The house itself was of oak and was covered with shingles, and there was glass for each of the twelve windows. The apartments of Ailill and Medb were in the centre of the house and had silver façades and strips of bronze; Ailill's façade had in it a silver wand that extended to the rafters of the house, and he used this to chastise the household. The warriors of Ulaid went round the house, from one door to the next and the musicians played while everything was being prepared. The house was so large that there was room for all the Ulaid to gather round Conchubur; Conchubur himself, however, and Fergus son of Roech and nine other Ulaid warriors gathered round Ailill's couch. A great feast was set out, and the visitors stayed three days and three nights.

Thereafter, Ailill inquired of Conchubur and the Ulaid why they had come, and Senchae explained the problem that had brought them: the rivalry of the three heroes for the champion's portion, the contention of the women over being first in to the feast, and how they would not suffer being judged by anyone but Ailill. Ailill fell silent at hearing that, and he was not happy. 'It would not be proper for me to give a judgement here,' he said, 'unless I were to do it out of hatred.' 'But no one is better qualified than you,' said Senchae. 'I would need some time to ponder the matter,' said Ailill. 'I expect three days and three nights would be enough.' 'No loss of friendship for that much time,' said Senchae.

Being satisfied, the Ulaid said farewell and took their leave of Ailill and Medb; they cursed Bricriu, for he had brought about this contention, and they returned to their own land, leaving behind Lóegure and Conall and Cú Chulaind to be judged by Ailill. That night, as the three heroes were being given their food, three cats, three druidic beasts, were loosed from the cave of Crúachu. Lóegure and Conall left their food to the beasts and fled to the rafters of the house, and they remained there all night. Cú Chulaind did not budge when the beasts approached him; when one beast stretched its neck out to eat, Cú Chulaind dealt it a blow on the head, but his sword glided off as if the creature were made of stone. The cat settled itself, then, and Cú Chulaind neither ate nor slept until morning. At dawn, the cats left, and the heroes were found where they spent the night. 'Does this contest not suffice for judgement?' Ailill said. 'Not at all,' replied Lóegure and Conall, 'for it is not beasts that we fight but men.'

Ailill went to his chamber, then, and put his back against the wall, and he was troubled in his mind. The problem that had been brought to him was so perplexing that for three days and three nights he neither ate nor slept; finally, Medb said to him, 'You are a weakling. If you are a judge, then judge.' 'It is difficult to judge them,' replied Ailill, 'and wretched he who must.' 'It is not difficult at all,' said Medb, 'for Lóegure and Conall are as different as bronze and white gold, and Conall and Cú Chulaind are as different as white gold and red gold.'

Medb thought over her advice after that, whereupon she summoned Lóegure Búadach to her and said, 'Welcome, Lóegure! You deserve the champion's portion, and so we make you king over the warriors of Ériu from this time forth, and we give you the champion's portion and this bronze cup, with a bird of white gold at the bottom, to bear before all as a token of our judgement. Let no one see it until you appear in Conchubur's Cráebrúad at the end of the day, and then, when the champion's portion is set out, display your cup to the chiefs of Ulaid. The champion's portion will be yours, and no other Ulaid warrior will challenge you for it, for your cup will be a token of recognition to the Ulaid.' Then the cup, filled with undiluted wine, was given to Lóegure, and there, in the centre of the royal house, he drained it at a swallow. 'Now yours is the feast of a champion,' said Medb, 'and may you enjoy it one-hundred-fold for one hundred years before the youths of all Ulaid.'

Lóegure bade farewell, then, and Conall was called to the centre of the royal house in the same way. 'Welcome, Conall,' Medb said. 'You deserve the champion's portion', and she went on as she had with Lóegure, except that she gave him a cup of white gold with a golden bird at the bottom. It was filled with undiluted wine and given to Conall, and he drained it at a swallow, and Medb wished him the champion's portion of all Ulaid for one hundred years.

Conall bade farewell, then, and Cú Chulaind was summoned; a messenger went to him and said, 'Come and speak with the king and queen.' At the time, Cú Chulaind was playing fidchell with Lóeg. 'You mock me,' he said to the messenger. 'Try your lies on another fool', and he threw a fidchell piece at the man so that it entered the brain; the messenger returned to Ailill and Medb and fell dead between them. 'Alas! Cú Chulaind will slaughter us if he is aroused,' said Medb. She rose, then, and went to Cú Chulaind and put her arm round his neck. 'Try another lie,' he said. 'Glorious lad of Ulaid, flame of the warriors of Ériu, we tell you no lies,' Medb replied. 'Were the choice of the warriors of Ériu to come, it is to you we would grant precedence, for the men of Ériu acknowledge your superiority, and that by reason of your youth and beauty, your courage and valour, your fame and renown.'

Cú Chulaind rose, then, and accompanied Medb to the royal house, and Ailill welcomed him warmly. He was given a cup of red gold with a bird of precious stone at the bottom, and it was filled with excellent wine; moreover, he was given the equivalent of two dragon's eyes. 'Now yours is the feast of a champion,' said Medb, 'and may you enjoy it one-hundred-fold for one hundred years before the youths of all Ulaid.' Ailill and Medb added, 'It is our judgement, moreover, that, just as no Ulaid youth is your equal, so no Ulaid woman is the equal of your wife, and it is our pleasure that Emer always be the first woman of Ulaid to enter the drinking house.' Cú Chulaind drained the cup at one swallow, bade farewell to king and queen and household, and followed Lóegure and Conall.

'My plan now,' Medb said to Ailill, 'is to keep the three heroes with us tonight, in order to test them further.' 'Do as

71

you like,' replied Ailill. The heroes were detained, then; their horses were unyoked, and they were taken to Crúachu. They were given a choice of food for their horses: Lóegure and Conall chose two-year-old oats, but Cú Chulaind asked for barley. The heroes slept at Crúachu that night, and the women were apportioned among them: Findabair and her fifty women were taken to Cú Chulaind's house, Sadb Sulbair (the other daughter of Ailill and Medb) and her fifty women were taken to Conall, and Conchend daughter of Cet son of Mágu and her fifty women were taken to Lóegure.

The next morning, the heroes rose early and went to the house where the lads were performing the wheel feat. Lóegure took the wheel and threw it halfway up the wall of the house; the lads laughed and smiled in mockery, but it seemed to Lóegure that they had raised a shout of victory. Conall then lifted the wheel from the floor and threw it up to the ridge pole of the royal house; the lads raised a shout of mockery, but Conall thought it a shout of applause and triumph. Cú Chulaind, however, caught the wheel in mid-air and threw it so high that it knocked the ridge pole from the house and sank into the ground outside the length of a man's arm; the lads raised a shout of praise and victory, but Cú Chulaind thought it a laugh of scorn and ridicule. After that, he went to the women and took their needles from them, and he threw the three fifties of needles into the air one after another; each needle went into the eye of the next, so that they all formed a chain. Afterwards, he returned each needle to its owner, and the lads praised him for that.

The three heroes bade farewell to the king and the queen and the rest of the household. 'Go to the house of my foster-father and foster-mother, Ercol and Garmuin,' said Medb, 'and be their guests tonight.' The three left after the horse-racing at the fair of Crúachu, where Cú Chulaind was victorious three times; they arrived at the house of Ercol and Garmuin and were welcomed. 'Why have you come?' Ercol asked. 'That you might judge us,' they replied. 'Go to the house of Samera, for it is he who will judge you,' Ercol said.

They left and were directed to Samera, and he welcomed them. Moreover, his daughter Búan fell in love with Cú Chulaind. They told Samera that they had come to him for judgement, and he sent them out, one by one, to the spectres of the air. Lóegure went first, but he left his weapons and clothing and fled. Conall went out in the same fashion, but he left his spears and his sword behind. Cú Chulaind went the third night. The spectres screeched at him and attacked; they shattered his spear and broke his shield and tore his clothing, and they bound and subdued him. 'Shame, Cú Chulaind,' said Lóeg, 'hapless weakling, one-eyed stripling, where are your skills and valour when spectres can destroy you?' At that, Cú Chulaind's ríastarthae overcame him, and he turned against the spectres; he tore them apart and crushed them, so that the air was full of their blood. Then he took their military cloaks and their weapons and returned triumphant to the house of Samera. Samera welcomed him and said, 'It is my judgement that the champion's portion should go to Cú Chulaind, that his wife should enter before all the women of Ulaid, and that his weapons should hang above the weapons of all others save those of Conchubur.'

After that, the three heroes returned to the house of Ercol, and he welcomed them, and they slept there that night. Ercol then announced that they would face himself and his horse. Lóegure and his horse went first: Ercol's gelding killed Lóegure's horse, and Ercol likewise prevailed over Lóegure, who fled, taking the road over Ess Rúaid to Emuin and reporting there that Ercol had killed his two companions. Conall fled in the same way after his horse had been killed by Ercol's gelding; en route to Emuin he crossed Snám Rathaind, and there his lad, Rathand, drowned in the river, and that is why the place is called Snám Rathaind.

The Líath Machae, however, killed Ercol's gelding, while Cú Chulaind overcame Ercol and bound him behind his chariot and drove off to Emuin Machae. Búan daughter of Samera followed the three chariots; she recognized the track of Cú Chulaind's chariot, for it left no narrow trail and moreover dug up walls and extended itself to leap over chasms. The girl made a fearful spring after the chariot; she struck her head against a rock and died, and thereafter the place was called Úaig Búana. In time, Conall and Cú Chulaind reached Emuin Machae, and they found the Ulaid in mourning, for, according to the report that Lóegure had brought back, the two of them had been killed. They related their news and adventures to Conchubur and the chieftains of Ulaid, and everyone reproached Lóegure for the false report he had brought back.

The youths left off their talk and their chatter, then, for their feast was set out, and that night it was Cú Chulaind's father himself, Súaltaim son of Roech, who served them. Their food was brought to them, and the distributors began to distribute but first they set the champion's portion aside. 'Why not give the champion's portion to one of the other heroes?' asked Dubthach Dóeltenga. 'After all, the three yonder would not have returned from Crúachu without some token showing that the champion's portion should be awarded to one of them.' At that, Lóegure Búadach rose and brandished his bronze cup with the silver bird at the bottom and said, 'Mine the champion's portion – therefore, let no one challenge me for it.' 'Not yours at all,' said Conall Cernach, 'for our tokens are not alike: you have brought a cup of bronze, but I have brought a cup of white gold. It is clear from the difference between them that the champion's portion is mine.' 'It belongs to neither of you,' said Cú Chulaind, and he rose and said, 'You have brought no token that merits the champion's portion. The king and queen of Crúachu were reluctant to arouse further hostility among us; nevertheless, you received from them only what you deserved. The champion's portion is mine, for it is I who have brought the most distinguished token.'

Cú Chulaind then brandished his cup of red gold with its bird of precious stone at the bottom, and he showed his equivalent of two dragon's eyes so that all the chieftains gathered round Conchubur could see. 'If there is any justice, it is I who should receive the champion's portion,' he concluded. 'We award it to you,' said Conchubur and Fergus and the other chieftains, 'for the champion's portion is yours, by the judgement of Ailill and Medb.' 'I swear by what my people swear by,' said Lóegure, 'that cup that you have brought was bought with jewels and treasures. You purchased your cup from Ailill and Medb so that you might not be disgraced and so that the champion's portion might not be given to anyone else.' 'I swear by the god my people swear by,' said Conall

Cernach, 'the judgement you have brought back is no judgement, and the champion's portion will not be yours.' At that, each of the three rose up with naked swords; Conchubur and Fergus stepped between them, then, and they sheathed their swords at once and sat down. 'Let my will prevail,' said Senchae. 'We agree to that,' they said. 'Then go to the ford of Bude son of Bain, and he will judge you,' said Senchae.

The three went to the house of Bude, then, and told him of the contention over which they had come and of their wish for a judgement. 'Was a judgement not given to you by Ailill and Medb at Crúachu?' Bude asked. 'Indeed, it was, but yonder men did not accept it,' said Cú Chulaind. 'Indeed, we do not,' said Lóegure and Conall, 'for the judgement that was given was no judgement at all.' 'Not easy for anyone to judge those who will not accept the judgement of Ailill and Medb,' said Bude. 'But I have someone who will undertake to judge you – Úath son of Imoman, who lives by the lake. Go to him, and he will decide.' This Úath son of Imoman was a man of great power: he could change into any form he wished, and he could perform druidry and discharge claims of mutual obligation. He was the spectre after which Belach Muni in tSiriti was named, and he was called a spectre because of his ability to transform himself into any shape.

The heroes went to Úath's lake, then, and Bude accompanied them as a witness. They told Úath why they had come; he replied that he would undertake to judge them but that they would have to accept his judgement. They agreed to accept it, and he took their pledges. Then he said, 'I propose a bargain, and he who fulfils it with me is he who will bear off the champion's portion.' 'What sort of bargain?' they asked. 'I have an axe,' he replied. 'Let one of you take it in his hand and cut off my head today, and I will cut off his head tomorrow.'

Lóegure and Conall said that they would not undertake that bargain, for, though he might have the power to remain alive after being beheaded, they did not. Thus, they refused the bargain. (Other books say, however, that they accepted the proposal: Lóegure cut the man's head off the first day but avoided him thereafter, and Conall did the same.) Cú Chulaind, however, said that he would undertake the bargain so that the champion's portion might be his. Lóegure and Conall said that, if he fulfilled that bargain with Úath, they would not contest his right to the champion's portion, and he accepted their pledges. Then he pledged to fulfil the bargain. Úath stretched his neck out on a stone (after first casting spells in the edge of the blade), and Cú Chulaind took the axe and cut off his head. Úath rose, took his axe, put his head on his chest and returned to the lake.

The following day, Úath reappeared, and Cú Chulaind stretched out his neck out on the stone. Three times Úath drew the axe down on Cú Chulaind's neck, and each time the blade was reversed. 'Rise, Cú Chulaind,' he said, then, 'for you are king of the warriors of Ériu, and the champion's portion is yours, without contest.' The three heroes returned to Emuin after that, but Lóegure and Conall did not accept the judgement that had been given to Cú Chulaind, and so the same strife arose regarding the champion's portion. It was the advice of the Ulaid that the three go to Cú Ruí for judgement, and they agreed to that.

The following morning, then, the three heroes went to Cú

Ruí's stronghold; they unyoked their chariots at the entrance and went into the royal house and were welcomed by Bláthnait daughter of Mend, for she was Cú Ruí's wife. Cú Ruí himself was not there that night, but he had known that they were coming, and he had instructed his wife what to do with the heroes until he returned from Scythia. From the time that he took arms until his death, Cú Ruí never reddened his sword in Ériu, and the food of Ériu did not pass his lips once he had reached the age of seven, for Ériu could not contain his strength and valour and courage and pride and fame and supremacy. Bláthnait followed his instructions in washing and bathing the heroes, in serving them intoxicating drink and in providing them excellent beds; and the three men were greatly pleased. When it came time to go to bed, she said that one of them would have to watch over the stronghold each night until Cú Ruí returned and Cú Ruí had said that the watch should be taken in order of age. Whatever part of the world Cú Ruí might be in, he sang a spell over his stronghold each night; it would then revolve as swiftly as a mill wheel turns, so that its entrance was never found after sunset.

Lóegure Búadch went to watch the first night, for he was the eldest of the three. Towards morning, he saw a giant approaching out of the ocean from the west, from as far away as the eye could see. This giant was huge and ugly and terrifying; it seemed to Lóegure that he was as tall as the sky and that the glimmer of the sea was visible between his legs. He came towards Lóegure, and his fists were full of stripped oak trunks; each would have been a burden for a team of oxen, and they had not been cut with repeated blows, either — each trunk had been severed with just one blow of a sword.

The giant cast a trunk, but Lóegure let it go by; two or three more trunks were cast, but they did not even strike Lóegure's shield, much less Lóegure himself. Lóegure in turn cast his spear at the giant and also failed. After that, the giant stretched out his hand towards Lóegure; the hand was so large that it spanned three ridges that had been between the combatants when they were casting at each other, and it seized Lóegure. For all Lóegure's size and excellence, he fitted in the giant's grip like a one-year-old child, and the giant ground him between his palms the way a fidchell piece would be ground by mill stones. When Lóegure was half dead, the giant dropped him over the stronghold walls and into the ditch at the entrance to the royal house. Since there was no entrance into the stronghold, Conall Cernach and Cú Chulaind and the people inside thought that Lóegure had leapt over the stronghold wall as a challenge to the other heroes.

At the end of the following day, Conall Cernach went out to watch, for he was older than Cú Chulaind, and everything that had happened to Lóegure the previous night happened to him also. The third night, Cú Chulaind went out to watch, and it was that night that the Three Greys of Sescend Úairbéoil and the Three Cowherds of Brega and the Three Sons of Dornmár Céoil gathered to destroy the stronghold. It was also that night that, according to prophecy, the monster in the lake nearby would devour everything in the stronghold, both man and beast. Cú Chulaind watched through the night, then, and many evil things happened. At midnight, he heard a loud noise approaching. 'Who goes there?' he shouted. 'If friends, let them halt; if enemies, let them flee.' At that, the enemies raised a great shout; Cú Chulaind sprang at them, then, and

79

nine of them fell dead on the ground. He put their heads into his watch seat, but scarcely had he sat down to watch when another nine shouted at him. He killed three nines in all and made a single heap of their heads and goods.

Night was drawing to a close, and Cú Chulaind was sad and weary when he heard the lake rising up as if it were a heavy sea. Tired as he was, his ardour would not let him remain, so he went towards the great noise, and he saw the monster – it seemed to have risen thirty cubits above the lake. The monster leapt at the stronghold and opened its mouth so wide that one of the royal houses would have fitted in its gullet. At that, Cú Chulaind remembered his coursing feat, and, leaping into the air, he circled the beast as quickly as a winnowing sieve. Then he put one hand on the monster's neck and the other down its gullet; he tore out its heart and threw that in the ground, and the beast fell heavily from the air. Cú Chulaind then hacked away until he made mincemeat of the monster, and he took its head down and put it with the pile of other heads.

Dawn was drawing on, and Cú Chulaind was wretched and broken when he saw the giant coming towards him from the western sea, just as Lóegure and Conall had seen. 'A bad night for you,' said the giant. 'A worse one for you, churl!' said Cú Chulaind. At that, the giant cast a tree trunk, but Cú Chulaind let it go by; two or three more casts were made, but they did not strike even Cú Chulaind's shield, much less Cú Chulaind himself. Cú Chulaind in turn cast his spear at the giant and also failed. The giant then stretched out his hand to take Cú Chulaind in his grasp as he had taken the other two men, but Cú Chulaind performed the hero's salmon leap and his coursing feat, with his sword overhead, so that he was as swift as a hare, and he hovered in a circle like a mill wheel. 'My life is yours!' said the giant. 'My requests, then,' said Cú Chulaind. 'You will have them even as you breathe them,' said the giant. 'Supremacy over the warriors of Ériu from this time on and the champion's portion without contest and precedence for my wife over the women of Ulaid for ever,' said Cú Chulaind. 'You will have that,' said the giant. With that, he vanished, and Cú Chulaind did not know where he had gone.

Cú Chulaind then thought about the leap that his comrades had made over the stronghold wall, which was high and broad, for he assumed that Lóegure and Conall must have leapt it. He attempted the leap twice and failed twice. 'A shame all the trouble I have taken over the champion's portion, to see it pass from me through failing to make the leap the others made,' he said, and he mused over this folly. He sprang back from the stronghold the length of a spearcast, and he sprang forward to where he had been standing, so that his forehead just touched the wall. He leapt straight up so that he could see everything that was happening inside, and he descended so that he sank into the ground up to his knees. And he did not remove the dew from the grass, even with the ardour of his feeling and the vigour of his disposition and the extent of his valour. With the fury and the ríastarthae that overcame him, he finally leapt the stronghold wall, so that he landed at the entrance to the royal house. He went inside and heaved a great sigh, and Bláthnait said, 'Indeed, not a sigh of shame but a sigh after victory and triumph', for the daughter of the king of Inis Fer Falga knew of the trials Cú Chulaind had endured that night.

Not long after that, they saw Cú Ruí coming towards them in the house; he had the war gear of the three nines whom Cú Chulaind had killed, along with their heads and the head of the beast. After taking the heads from his chest and putting them in the centre of the house, he said, 'The lad who has collected all these trophies in one night is fit to watch over the stronghold of a king. That which they dispute, the champion's portion, truly belongs to Cú Chulaind in preference to every youth of Ériu, for none could meet him in combat.' Cú Ruí thus awarded the champion's portion to Cú Chulaind, naming him the most valorous of the Goídil and giving his wife precedence over the other women of Ulaid in entering the drinking house. Moreover, he gave Cú Chulaind seven cumals' worth of gold and silver as a reward for the deeds he had done that night.

The three heroes bade farewell to Cú Ruí, then, and returned to Emuin Machae before the end of the day. When it came time for the servers to divide and distribute, they removed the champion's portion and its drink and set them aside. 'We are certain that you will not be contesting the champion's portion tonight,' said Dubthach Dóeltenga, 'for you will have received judgement from him to whom you went.' But Lóegure and Conall said that the champion's portion had not been awarded to any of the three in preference to the others, and, as for the judgement of Cú Ruí upon the three, they said that he had awarded nothing at all to Cú Chulaind since they had reached Emuin Machae. Cú Chulaind then said that he would not contest the champion's portion, for the good of having it would be no greater than the trouble involved. Thus, the champion's portion was not awarded until after the warrior's bargain at Emuin Machae.

Once, when the Ulaid were at Emuin Machae, tired after the fair and the games, Conchubur and Fergus and the other Ulaid chieftains returned from the playing field to sit in Conchubur's Cráebrúad. Lóegure and Conall and Cú Chulaind were not there that evening, but the best of the other warriors of Ulaid were. As night drew on, they saw a huge, ugly churl coming towards them in the house, and it seemed to them that there was not in all Ulaid a warrior half as tall. His appearance was frightful and terrifying: a hide against his skin, and a dun cloak round him, and a great bushy tree overhead where a winter shed for thirty calves could fit. Each of his two yellow eyes was the size of an ox-cauldron; each finger was as thick as a normal man's wrist. The tree trunk in his left hand would have been a burden for twenty yoked oxen; the axe in his right hand, whence had gone three fifties of glowing metal pieces, had a handle that would have been a burden for a team of oxen, yet it was sharp enough to cut hairs against the wind.

He came in this guise and stood beneath the forked beam at one end of the fire. 'Do you find the house so narrow,' said Dubthach Dóeltenga, 'that there is no place to stand but under the forked beam? You may wish to contest the position of house candlebearer, but you are more likely to burn the house than to illuminate the company inside.'

'Although that is my gift,' the churl replied, 'perhaps you will grant that, despite my height, the entire household may be lit without the house's being burnt. But that is not my primary gift, and I have others. That which I have come to seek I have not found in Ériu or the Alps or Europe or Africa or Asia or Greece or Scythia or Inis Orc or the Pillars of Hercules or Tor mBregoind or Inis Gaid. Nowhere have I found a man to keep my bargain. Since you Ulaid surpass the hosts of every land in anger and prowess and weaponry, in rank and pride and dignity, in honour and generosity and excellence, let one of you keep faith with me in the matter over which I have come.'

'It is not right,' said Fergus, 'to dishonour a province because of one man's failure to keep his word – perhaps death is no nearer to him than it is to you.' 'It is not I who shirk death,' replied the churl. 'Then let us hear your proposal,' said Fergus. 'Only if I am allowed fair play,' said the churl. 'It is right to allow him that,' said Senchae son of Ailill, 'for it would be no fair play if a great host broke faith with a completely unknown individual. Besides, it would seem to us that if you are to find the man you seek, you will find him here.' 'I exempt Conchubur, for he is the king, and I exempt Fergus, for he is of equal rank,' said the churl. 'Whoever else may dare, let him come that I may cut off his head tonight, he mine tomorrow.'

'After those two,' said Dubthach, 'there is certainly no warrior here worthy of that.' 'Indeed, there is,' said Muinremur son of Gerrgend, and he sprang to the centre of the house. Now Muinremur had the strength of one hundred warriors, and each arm had the strength of one hundred. 'Bend down, churl,' he said, 'that I may cut off your head tonight – you may cut off mine tomorrow night.' 'I could make that bargain anywhere,' said the churl. 'Let us rather make the bargain I proposed: I will cut off your head tonight, and you will avenge that by cutting off my head tomorrow night.' 'I swear by what my people swear by,' said Dubthach Dóeltenga, 'such a death would not be pleasant if the man you killed tonight clung to you tomorrow. But you alone have the power to be killed one night and to avenge it the next.' 'Then whatever conditions you propose I will fulfil, surprising as you may find that,' said the churl, whereupon he made Muinremur pledge to keep his part of the bargain the following night.

With that, Muinremur took the churl's axe, whose two edges were seven feet apart. The churl stretched his neck out on the block, and Muinremur so swung the axe that it struck the block underneath; the head rolled to the foot of the forked beam, and the house was filled with blood. At once, the churl rose, gathered his head and his block and his axe and clutched then to his chest, and left the house, blood streaming from his neck and filling the Cráebruad on every side. The household were horrorstruck by the wondrousness of the event they had witnessed. 'I swear by what my people swear by,' said Dubthach Dóeltenga, 'if that churl returns tomorrow after having been killed tonight, not a man in Ulaid will be left alive.'

The following night, the churl returned but Muinremur avoided him. The churl complained, saying, 'Indeed, it is not fair of Muinremur to break his part of the bargain.' Lóegure Búadach, however, was present that night, and, when the churl continued, 'Who of the warriors who contest the champion's portion of Ulaid will fulfil this bargain with me tonight? Where is Lóegure Búadach?' Lóegure said, 'Here I am!' The churl pledged Lóegure as he had pledged Muinremur, but Lóegure, like Muinremur, failed to appear the following night. The churl then pledged Conall Cernach, and he too failed to appear and keep his pledge.

When he arrived on the fourth night, the churl was seething with rage. All the women of Ulaid had gathered there that night to see the marvel that had come to the Cráebrúad, and Cú Chulaind had come as well. The churl began to reproach them, saying, 'Men of Ulaid, your skill and courage are no more. Your warriors covet the champion's portion, yet they are unable to contest it. Where is that pitiful stripling you call Cú Chulaind? Would his word be better than that of his companions?' 'I want no bargain with you,' said Cú Chulaind. 'No doubt you fear death, wretched fly,' said the churl. At that, Cú Chulaind sprang towards the churl and dealt him such a blow with the axe that his head was sent to the rafters of the Cráebrúad, and the entire house shook. Cú Chulaind then struck the head with the axe once more, so that it shattered into fragments. The churl rose none the less.

The following day, the Ulaid watched Cú Chulaind to see if he would avoid the churl the way his companions had done; they saw that he was waiting for the churl, and they grew very dejected. It seemed to them proper to begin his death dirge, for they feared greatly that he would live only until the churl appeared. Cú Chulaind, ashamed, said to Conchubur, 'By my shield and by my sword, I will not go until I have fulfilled my pledge to the churl – since I am to die, I will die with honour.'

Towards the end of the day, they saw the churl approaching them. 'Where is Cú Chulaind?' he asked. 'Indeed, I am here,' said Cú Chulaind. 'You speak low, tonight, wretch, for you fear death greatly,' said the churl. 'Yet for all that, you have not avoided me.' Cú Chulaind rose and stretched his neck out on the block, but its size was such that his neck reached only halfway across. 'Stretch out your neck, you wretch,' said the churl. 'You torment me,' said Cú Chulaind. 'Kill me quickly. I did not torment you last night. Indeed, I swear, if you torment me now, I will make myself as long as a heron above you.' 'I cannot dispatch you, not with the length of the block and the shortness of your neck,' said the churl.

Cú Chulaind stretched himself, then, until a warrior's foot would fit between each rib, and he stretched his neck until it reached the other side of the block. The churl raised his axe so that it reached the rafters of the house. What with the creaking of the old hide that he wore and the swish of his axe as he raised it with the strength of his two arms, the sound he made was like that of a rustling forest on a windy night. The churl brought the axe down, then, upon Cú Chulaind's neck – with the blade turned up. All the chieftains of Ulaid saw this.

'Rise, Cú Chulaind!' the churl then said. 'Of all the warriors in Ulaid and Ériu, whatever their merit, none is your equal for courage and skill and honour. You are the supreme warrior of Ériu, and the champion's portion is yours, without contest; moreover, your wife will henceforth enter the drinking house before all the other women of Ulaid. Whoever might dispute this judgement, I swear by what my people swear by, his life will not be long.' After that, the churl vanished. It was Cú Ruí son of Dáre, who in that guise had come to fulfil the promise he had made to Cú Chulaind.

PENGUIN 60s CLASSICS

APOLLONIUS OF RHODES · *Jason and the Argonauts*
ARISTOPHANES · *Lysistrata*
SAINT AUGUSTINE · *Confessions of a Sinner*
JANE AUSTEN · *The History of England*
HONORÉ DE BALZAC · *The Atheist's Mass*
BASHŌ · *Haiku*
GIOVANNI BOCCACCIO · *Ten Tales from the Decameron*
JAMES BOSWELL · *Meeting Dr Johnson*
CHARLOTTE BRONTË · *Mina Laury*
CAO XUEQIN · *The Dream of the Red Chamber*
THOMAS CARLYLE · *On Great Men*
BALDESAR CASTIGLIONE · *Etiquette for Renaissance Gentlemen*
CERVANTES · *The Jealous Extremaduran*
KATE CHOPIN · *The Kiss*
JOSEPH CONRAD · *The Secret Sharer*
DANTE · *The First Three Circles of Hell*
CHARLES DARWIN · *The Galapagos Islands*
THOMAS DE QUINCEY · *The Pleasures and Pains of Opium*
DANIEL DEFOE · *A Visitation of the Plague*
BERNAL DÍAZ · *The Betrayal of Montezuma*
FYODOR DOSTOYEVSKY · *The Gentle Spirit*
FREDERICK DOUGLASS · *The Education of Frederick Douglass*
GEORGE ELIOT · *The Lifted Veil*
GUSTAVE FLAUBERT · *A Simple Heart*
BENJAMIN FRANKLIN · *The Means and Manner of Obtaining Virtue*
EDWARD GIBBON · *Reflections on the Fall of Rome*
CHARLOTTE PERKINS GILMAN · *The Yellow Wallpaper*
GOETHE · *Letters from Italy*
HOMER · *The Rage of Achilles*
HOMER · *The Voyages of Odysseus*

PENGUIN 60s CLASSICS

ANONYMOUS WORKS

READ MORE IN PENGUIN

For complete information about books available from Penguin and how to order them, please write to us at the appropriate address below. Please note that for copyright reasons the selection of books varies from country to country.

IN THE UNITED KINGDOM: Please write to *Dept. JC, Penguin Books Ltd, FREEPOST, West Drayton, Middlesex UB7 OBR.*

If you have any difficulty in obtaining a title, please send your order with the correct money, plus ten per cent for postage and packaging, to *PO Box No. 11, West Drayton, Middlesex UB7 OBR.*

IN THE UNITED STATES: Please write to *Consumer Sales, Penguin USA, P.O. Box 999, Dept. 17109, Bergenfield, New Jersey 07621-0120.* VISA and MasterCard holders call 1-800-253-6476 to order all Penguin titles.

IN CANADA: Please write to *Penguin Books Canada Ltd, 10 Alcorn Avenue, Suite 300, Toronto, Ontario M4V 3B2.*

IN AUSTRALIA: Please write to *Penguin Books Australia Ltd, P.O. Box 257, Ringwood, Victoria 3134.*

IN NEW ZEALAND: Please write to *Penguin Books (NZ) Ltd, Private Bag 102902, North Shore Mail Centre, Auckland 10.*

IN INDIA: Please write to *Penguin Books India Pvt Ltd, 706 Eros Apartments, 56 Nehru Place, New Delhi 110 019.*

IN THE NETHERLANDS: Please write to *Penguin Books Netherlands bv, Postbus 3507, NL-1001 AH Amsterdam.*

IN GERMANY: Please write to *Penguin Books Deutschland GmbH, Metzlerstrasse 26, 60594 Frankfurt am Main.*

IN SPAIN: Please write to *Penguin Books S. A., Bravo Murillo 19, 1° B, 28015 Madrid.*

IN ITALY: Please write to *Penguin Italia s.r.l., Via Felice Casati 20, I-20124 Milano.*

IN FRANCE: Please write to *Penguin France S. A., 17 rue Lejeune, F-31000 Toulouse.*

IN JAPAN: Please write to *Penguin Books Japan, Ishikiribashi Building, 2-5-4, Suido, Bunkyo-ku, Tokyo 112.*

IN GREECE: Please write to *Penguin Hellas Ltd, Dimocritou 3, GR-106 71 Athens.*

IN SOUTH AFRICA: Please write to *Longman Penguin Southern Africa (Pty) Ltd, Private Bag X08, Bertsham 2013.*